Orlando Ghost Story

Maria DiFrancesco

Kindle Direct Publishing

Contents

Chapter 1

October is here. Sandy loves autumn, and October is her favorite month. Her best friend, Rita, and Rita's husband, Kevin, have an annual Halloween party at their big old house in Catonsville Maryland. Sandy and her husband, Dominic, look forward to it every year. Dom hates dressing up in a costume, though, so Sandy must think of a clever theme for the two of them and talk him into wearing coordinating get-ups.

She's getting into the mood by decorating her old house in Ellicott City for the season. Sandy found some cute lights at Walmart that she is using to decorate her roof top garden. She bought a few strings with orange jack-o-lanterns, and a few with white ghosts, and is stringing them onto the bushes. Timmy, her fat gray tabby, is 'helping' by swatting at the strings and chasing leaves across the roof deck. She also bought some pots of yellow, orange, and purple mums to decorate the space for fall, since her petunias and snapdragons have just had their last hurrah for the season. Sandy breathes in the fresh air and admires how crisp and clean everything looks on this sunny day with no humidity.

Despite her love of fall, she dreads the short days and lack of sunshine that are part of winter. Sandy finds that Christmas lights in the house help her to feel happier on the dark nights, so she decides to put up a Halloween tree this year to get the spirit going even sooner.

Mr. Tim follows her back into the house and down into the basement, watching as she drags out the artificial Christmas tree. Timmy loves all trees, real or artificial, and is excitedly waiting as Sandy sets the tree up in the living room. As soon as it is standing, he finds a spot underneath the tree and curls up for a nap.

"Hey, little buddy, I still need to put the lights and the decorations on!" she tells the cat. He blinks his eyes open for a moment, lets out a little chortle, then immediately resumes his nap. Walmart also had orange and purple light strings, and some cute Halloween ornaments, so she bought them for decorating the tree. She even found a witch to put on top.

Sandy finishes decorating without disturbing the kitty too much, plugs in the lights, and takes a look. "Perfect!" she says to herself.

"Yes, it is!" Dominic says from behind her.

Sandy jumps. "I didn't know you were home. You scared me!"

"Sorry sweetie," Dom says as he pulls her in for a kiss. "What's that lazy cat doing?"

"Helping me decorate. Hey, you are sweaty!" she says as she pushes him away from her. "How was your bike ride with Kevin?"

"Tiring!" Dom says. "We did 75 miles, which is the farthest we have gone so far. We're working our way up to the full Ironman distance in Panama City next year. We will ride 112 miles for that race. And that's after swimming 2.4 miles!"

"And then you run a marathon afterward...I don't know how anyone does that! Or why any sane person would want to."

"Well, I've done the half Ironman before, and the training guides say it's more about knowing how to consume the right number of calories than it is about training longer and harder when you move up to the longer distances."

"I'm sure you will do great. I'm proud of you, and we will be happy to cheer you on with an adult beverage in hand!" Sandy is not an athlete by any stretch of the imagination. Doing any part of the swim, bike, or run sounds like torture to her.

"You and Rita will have fun together in Panama City while we are grinding through it. My goal is to complete the race in under 11.5 hours. Kevin is shooting for 12.5 hours since he's only done a sprint distance race in the past. But he has run several marathons, so the run will be the easiest leg for him."

"Like I said, we'll be cheering you on from the

sidelines!"

"I'm going to shower, care to join me?" Dom asks with a grin as he heads up the stairs.

"That's an invitation I can't pass up!" Sandy says as she bounds up the stairs after him.

Chapter 2

Dom and Sandy are en route to Rita and Kevin's house in Catonsville for the Halloween bash. It's always so much fun that Dom didn't fuss too much about putting on the costume that Sandy came up with. They've been watching *Our Flag Means Death*, the TV series about Stede Bonnet, AKA the Gentleman Pirate, and Blackbeard, whose real name was Edward Teach. The two of them are historic figures who met in 1717 and did collaborate as pirates. Sandy is dressed as Stede, who was quite the dandy, in a lacy white shirt and a turquoise jacket with large buttons and fancy trim. She's wearing a red wig and a red handlebar mustache since Stede was a redhead. Blackbeard, who also had the reputation of being a snappy dresser, enjoyed wearing make-up, so Sandy went heavy with the eyeliner on Dominic. He grumbled a bit about the long black wig and black beard, but Sandy thinks he looks super sexy in it. The costume includes a black leather jacket and a sword and scabbard around his waist. With his broad shoulders and athletic build, Dom is totally rocking it.

There are a dozen cars in front of the house

when they pull up and park. Purple and orange lights decorate the trees and bushes in front of the old mansion, which was built in the 1920s, and several ghosts and ghouls decorate the wraparound porch. The beautiful wooden staircase in the foyer is strung with more purple and orange lights. People are gathered in the living room and dining room on either side of the stairs talking and enjoying the bounty of drinks and snacks that Rita has arranged on the large dining table. Tutti winds around Sandy's legs, and she leans down to pet her.

"Hey little girl! How are you doing? Mr. Tim misses you. You two need to have a playdate soon." Rita and Sandy take turns babysitting the cats when either of them is away on travel, and Tutti and Tim are great friends. Right now, Tutti looks overwhelmed by all the people, and she scampers off to a quieter room.

Rita comes over to greet them. "You two look awesome! Stede Bonnet and Blackbeard, right? We love that show." Rita grabs Sandy and gives her a huge hug, then moves on to give Dom a squeeze. Rita calls across the room to Kevin, "Come over here, honey! Sandy and Dom are here." Rita loves the roaring twenties and is appropriately clad in a flapper dress and a feathered band around her head. Kevin ambles over to join her wearing a pinstriped suit, gangster hat, and toting a shotgun.

"You two look amazing!" Sandy says. "Let me get a pic!" She pulls out her phone and snaps a few photos as Rita and Kevin willingly pose for her. Rita grabs the camera and takes a few shots of Sandy and Dom.

"Text those to me later, girlfriend!" Rita tells Sandy.

"Sure will! Where's little Davey tonight?" Davey is Rita and Kevin's 2-year-old son.

"Kevin's mom is watching him tonight. She's keeping James, too, and the two of them always have a ball together," Rita tells her.

"Is Stacey here tonight?" Sandy asks. Stacey is Kevin's sister, and James is her son.

"Yes, she's over there in the Oompa Loompa costume. Chad is with her – he's dressed as Willy Wonka." Sandy looks over and sees that Chad, Stacey's partner, is wearing a long, bright pink coat and a brown top hat. Stacey's face is painted orange, her eyebrows are white, and she's wearing a bright green wig.

"They look great!" Sandy says.

"Yeah, aren't they cute together?" Rita asks. "Hey, can you help me gather all the guests – we made a haunted passageway through the house, using the hidden staircase and the tunnel under the basement." Rita and Kevin discovered their old house's secrets when they were doing renovations shortly after they purchased the place.

"Sure! That sounds like fun. I just hope you didn't disturb any ghosts in the process," Sandy tells her.

"No, we haven't had any more ghosts since you helped us with Kelly two years ago."

Sandy is very sensitive to spiritual energy, and if there are ghosts in the vicinity, they will be attracted to her. She knows from experience that most of them are looking for something – trying to resolve some unfinished business from their life. Once they take care of that business, they can move on to the spiritual realm.

Rita has the guests, excluding anyone who knows about the secret passageways in the house, divide into two teams for a haunted scavenger hunt. Dom and Sandy helped Kevin and Rita do the renovations on their house after they moved in, so they know the house's secrets and are excluded from the game, but will happily watch the two teams try to figure out the clues.

"I'm going to grab a beer to enjoy during the hunt. Do you want anything?" Dom asks his wife.

"Yes, grab me a black cherry White Claw. Thanks!"

The hidden staircase can be accessed through the closet in the foyer on the first floor, or from a closet in the master bedroom on the second floor. There are scavenger hunt clues scattered around the house that could take them in either way, depending on which hint they find first. Sandy and Dom are sticking with Team 1, and they are digging around in the foyer closet trying to find the false back that swings open to the staircase. Rita and Kevin are with Team 2, who are upstairs poking around in the master bedroom.

Sandy hears people talking and laughing coming down the back staircase, so she knows Team 2 found the way in. The noise spurs Team 1 on and they quickly find the latch that opens the door in the foyer closet and pull it open in time to see the last of Team 2 going by. There are purple lights lining the entire narrow staircase, and casting an eerie glow on the ghosts and ghouls that have been strategically placed along the way.

"This is so creepy!" Sandy says. Dom tickles the back of her neck lightly with his fingers, and she screams. "Quit that!" she laughs. Her scream was enough to startle a few other guests, who screamed after she did.

When they get to the basement at the bottom of the stairs, the space is dimly lit and there are cobwebs everywhere, inhabited by huge plastic spiders with large fangs. A bat flies from one wall to the other, eliciting another round of shrieks from the guests. As they walk further into the room, they approach a graveyard filled with tombstones. Each one has the name of one of the guests on it, with the same date of death for each of them – today's date – along with a funny inscription regarding the cause of death for each of them. Sandy, whose love for her fat cat is well known by the whole friend group, expired from being smothered with love by Mr. Tim. Dominic met his end on a poorly marked triathlon course, where he rode his expensive bike off a cliff. Kevin, ever the competitive one and thinking it was a shortcut, followed Dominic off the same cliff. Their times of death were 30 seconds apart.

"This is a bit morbid," Dom tells Sandy.

"It's all in good fun," she whispers back.

The next clue, which both teams find at about the same time, on a sign being held by a skeleton who is guarding the graveyard gate, says, "11:59:59." Team 1 quickly realizes that this is the time of death that is listed on Rita's tombstone. Rita loves fireworks, and her tombstone gives the reason for her demise as using too short a wick when lighting a pack of colorful explosives. They investigate the tombstone and find the last clue hidden underneath it. The hint leads them to a button behind a support post. Someone pushes it, and what looked like a cement wall is a well camouflaged garage door that mechanically rolls up and opens a passageway. At the end of the passageway, about 20 feet ahead, is an iron gate, which is locked, but there is more of the tunnel past the gate. In front of the gate is a large trophy, which Team 1 claims, and a nice basket of assorted airplane liquor bottles in lots of varieties.

The guests have many questions about this hidden space under the house. Rita explains that the tunnels were used as part of the Underground Railroad years ago. Kevin tells them that the tunnels lead to another house and a nearby warehouse, and he put the iron gate in place to keep people from wandering into their home from the connecting tunnels. Tutti gives them all a scare as she suddenly jumps out from the corner and sprints up the stairs. They all scream, then laugh, then head back upstairs to enjoy more food, drinks, and conversation.

Chapter 3

The past few months have been extraordinarily busy for Sandy after being assigned to a new project at the Applied Physics Laboratory where she works. She doesn't mind, though, because she has been trying to get on Project Dragonfly for a while. The objective is to study Titan, the largest moon of Saturn, to evaluate the feasibility of building an Earth colony there. Titan is the largest of Saturn's 146 moons and is the only one in our solar system that has an atmosphere thick enough to protect against radiation, an ample supply of natural gas to power a civilization, and an abundant amount of ice that could be converted to water. The Dragonfly team will develop a nuclear powered, car-sized drone to collect and evaluate samples collected from Titan. The drone is a rotorcraft-lander and must operate at temperatures down to -180 degrees Celsius and in an atmosphere 3.5 times as dense as Earth's atmosphere. APL has many partners on the project, including NASA, Lockheed Martin, and Penn State, as well as German, French, and Japanese space agencies.

Sandy's background is in biology, and she is

working on the team that is developing the processes and equipment needed for analyzing the samples in the Dragonfly mass spectrometer. It's all very exciting, and the team has the goal of reaching launch readiness by July of 2028, which is just four years away. She enjoys the work and loves attending the quarterly all-hands meetings where she can see the big picture and understand where her small piece fits into the overarching project.

Sandy is normally all in for the Christmas holidays, but long workdays have put her behind in her preparations. It's already December 15 and she hasn't put up a single decoration or bought any presents. She's embarrassed that her Halloween tree is still up. She'd be even more stressed out if she and Dominic hadn't already decided to keep the gifts to each other to a minimum and put their money into a renovation for their home, which Dom is handling. They are finishing the basement and installing a hot tub and a sauna. Dom already has his treadmill and bike trainer down there in the unfinished area, but it will be a lot nicer when they get it fixed up. Since Sandy and Dom helped with the renovations on Rita and Kevin's house, they are happy to return the favor and give Dom a hand. Kevin is training with Dominic for the Ironman triathlon in November and has every intention of taking advantage of the sauna and hot tub to loosen up his tight muscles after a grueling workout with Dominic, who talked him into this insanity in the first place. Sandy, who has no plans of ever doing a triathlon, loves a hot tub and a sauna, and is looking forward to using both even with no sore muscles.

The night is so dark as Sandy pulls into her driveway at 7 PM that she vows to herself that she is going to get the outside lights up this weekend. The short days in the winter negatively affect her mood, and the lights go a long way in cheering things up. Right now, it's dark in the morning when she leaves for work, and dark when she gets in her car to drive home in the evening. And she hasn't been good about taking a break at lunchtime to at least walk around outside to get some sunshine. The lack of sunlight is taking its toll on her. The forecast for Saturday is sunny and not too cold, so it will be a perfect time to put up lights and enjoy the sun.

Timmy rushes to the door to greet Sandy as she enters the kitchen. "Hey, buddy!" she says as she reaches down to swoop him up into a bear hug. He tolerates her kisses for half a minute, then squirms to get down. "Didn't your Papa feed you?" she says as she glances at his empty food bowl.

Dominic is at the stove fixing steak sandwiches for them for dinner. "He had his dinner! The little pig scarfed it all up already," Dom tells her. "I'm making steak sandwiches with bulgogi barbecue sauce. I cut up some purple cabbage to put on top."

"Yum, that sounds great!" Sandy says. "Thanks for cooking and taking care of Mr. Tim." She looks down at the cat, who is still staring up at her.

"Meow!"

"Don't try to trick me, kitty. I know you were already fed!" The cat wanders away. Sandy swears that he understands most of what they say to him.

Sandy gets two Bud Lights out of the fridge and puts one down at Dom's place at the table as he carries their plated sandwiches over. Sandy takes a bite. "This is delicious! Thanks, sweetie."

"Glad you like it! I like the bulgogi flavor on the steak and the cabbage gives it a nice crunch."

"Yeah, it's good. Did you talk to the contractor today? When can they start on the basement?"

"Yep, I did. He has a few jobs to finish up before the holidays, so they can't do it until the first week in January," he tells her.

"Oh, darn. I know you really wanted to get the hot tub and sauna in place so you could enjoy them during your holiday break."

"That would have been nice, but I knew it was an aggressive schedule. You'll just have to give me leg massages until then!" Dom grins. Sandy gives her husband a leg massage most Saturdays. She teases him that he is the most privileged husband around.

"You are so spoiled!" Sandy laughs.

"What's wrong with that? You are supposed to spoil your husband."

"I suppose I am." Sandy smiles and knows she's lucky to have Dom to spoil. He does a good job of spoiling her, too.

Chapter 4

The holidays flew by in a blur – it's already New Year's Eve and time to ring in the coming year. Dominic surprised Sandy with a kitten for Christmas. She had been telling him for the past few months that they should get another cat. Mr. Tim is a very social kitty, and he hates being at home by himself when the two of them work long hours, which seems to be the case more and more often lately. Timmy took to Rita's cat, Tutti, immediately and they have playdates often when Rita and Sandy cat-sit for each other. Dominic made a lot of excuses about why they shouldn't get another pet – the cats might not get along, they already don't have time for one cat, so it doesn't make sense to get another, and they both love to travel, so having more pets to look after just makes that harder. Sandy was disappointed but couldn't really argue with the points that Dom made.

When the doorbell rang at 9 AM on Christmas morning, Sandy was confused about who would be coming to the door this early on a holiday. Dom went to answer it, then called out to Sandy that she had a visitor. When she went to the door, Rita was there holding a wicker picnic basket, like the one that Toto was shoved into in the Wizard of Oz. Little Davey was standing beside her.

"Dominic wants me to deliver this gift for him," Rita said as she handed the basket to Sandy.

"It's a kitten!" Davey shouted.

"You weren't supposed to tell the secret, honey!" Rita laughed. The kitten was meowing so Sandy opened the lid and lifted out the cutest little black and white tuxedo cat you can imagine.

"He is so adorable!" Sandy said, and glanced at Dom. "But you said we shouldn't get another cat!"

Dominic grinned at her. "Pretty good acting, yeah?"

Sandy kissed the kitten and then Dom. "I love him! I'm going to name him Maceo."

"Maceo? Why?" Dominic asked.

"That's a Jane's Addiction song," Rita told him. "Maceo was Perry Ferrell's cat. Great song!"

Dominic frowned, like that was the stupidest name he had ever heard, but said, "Whatever you want, Sandy. He's your cat."

After only a week, the two cats are getting along famously. Right now, they are napping - Maceo is curled up in a little ball with Timmy's body encircled around him and his paw on top of him. It's so adorable that Sandy feels compelled to get out her phone and take a couple pics.

"You have twice as many photos of those cats as you do anything else!" Dom fusses, but Sandy knows he's a kibitzer and loves them just as much as she does.

"You cats better get your naps in now," Sandy says. "We're having a party tonight and it's going to be loud in here!"

They decided to stay home to celebrate New Year's Eve and invited about twenty of their friends over. One of the engineers that Sandy works with at APL, Devin, is the guitarist for a band, Mama Boy, with three of his buddies. They play a lot of covers and write their own music as well, and they agreed to play for beer, food, and a place to spend the night. Sandy's old house is huge, with four bedrooms on the second floor, and two more bedrooms in the attic, plus sofas and air mattresses. Anyone who is planning on drinking tonight will have a place to sleep.

Sandy has plenty of food and drinks for the party, but everyone shows up with booze, snacks, and desserts in hand, so the spread across the kitchen counter, island, and table is fit for a king. Sandy made her famous crab dip, which is a big hit, and Dom just took the sourdough bread bowl full of melted brie out of the oven, and people are digging in with crackers and toasted bread cubes and telling her how delicious it is. In addition, there is a crockpot full of meatballs, a veggie tray, a plate full of Italian meats, cheeses, and olives, chips, pretzels, dips, salsa, guacamole, and a myriad of cookies, cakes, and pies. No one will go hungry tonight.

Timmy and Maceo, enjoying all the extra petting and attention, are very friendly with the guests. They hang out at the party until Mama Boy starts tuning up their instruments, then they turn tail and head up the stairs to hide in one of the bedrooms. Mama Boy plays several covers, mixed in with their original songs, which are quite good. They play two 1-hour sets, with a 30-minute break in between.

It's approaching midnight, so they make their way outside to get ready for the 'Crab Drop', which is Dominic's version of the Ball Drop at Times Square in New York City. Baltimore has the best hard-shell crabs in the world, so it's very fitting that their drop will honor the tasty crustacean. It's cold out, around 30 degrees, so everyone is bundled in their coats and scarves, waiting for the countdown. Devin brings a Bluetooth speaker out and hooks it to his phone so he can play Prince's 1999, the perfect New Year's Eve party countdown song. The large plastic crab, sparkling with red and gold lights, waits at the top of the flagpole as the countdown commences. The guests all shout '10 – 9 – 8 – 7 – 6 – 5 – 4 – 3 – 2 – 1!' The crab descends on the flag rope right on cue. Devin quickly switches the music to Auld Lang Syne. The guests kiss, hug, and sing along to the song, then quickly make a dash into the house to get warm again.

Chapter 5

Sandy is fed up with winter and it is only February! It's been rainy, then snowy, then very cold. Workdays for both her and Dominic have been brutally long. She is feeling depressed, cranky, and weighed down by the lack of sunlight. She's even been snapping at Dominic for no reason, which he doesn't need, since work has been taking a toll on him as well.

When Sandy's team leader at APL told her that he wanted her to go to Florida to work with the Project Dragonfly partners at NASA and Lockheed Martin, she had to restrain herself from giving him a big hug. She will be there for a month, so she rented a pet friendly AirBNB townhouse so that Timmy and Maceo could come along. Neither one of them has been on a long trip in the car, so she doesn't know what to expect, but the vet gave her some pills that will help reduce their anxiety. Because of his work schedule, Dominic will not be able to come to Florida for a month, but he can come for a week and work remotely. He's not happy that she is taking both cats with her, but she can't imagine being away from them for a month, especially Timmy. She's had him since he was a kitten – she got him years before she met Dom.

The car is loaded up and all that is left to do is pack up the cats. Sandy remembers the Local H album, *Pack Up the Cats,* that her mom played a lot when she was little. Her mom and dad listened to a lot of hard rock when she was young. Green Day was another one of their favorites. They were listening to *Brainstew* on the way into daycare when Sandy was little, and her 'teacher' was horrified when she started singing 'my eyes feel like they're gonna bleed.' Her mom quickly explained that they were lyrics to the Green Day song, Brainstew, and that there was nothing wrong with Sandy's eyes.

The vet gave Sandy a prescription for Gabapentin to give the cats to reduce their anxiety while riding in the car. Since Maceo is so small, he just needs half a pill. Fat Mr. Tim needs two pills. She uses a 'pill popper' syringe to shoot the pills in their mouths, and holds their jaws shut while blowing on their faces to get them to swallow. Dominic holds them down while she is trying to get the pills into them. Timmy tricks her by holding the pill at the side of his mouth, then spitting it on the floor when she puts him down. She checks his mouth before putting him down after the next two pills.

The vet told Sandy that it takes up to two hours for the medicine to take effect. She can see that they are acting woozy after an hour and a half, so she puts them each in a cat carrier and Dominic helps her carry them out to the car and load them

23

into the pet tunnel that spans the width of the back seat. The cats have room to move around and use the small litterbox that Sandy placed at the far end of the tunnel. Their favorite fuzzy blanket is at the other end of the tunnel for them to sleep on. She kisses Dominic, puts the Hampton Inn in Santee, South Carolina into her GPS, and finds the *Pack Up the Cats* album on Spotify and hits play. The drive will take eight hours, including a couple quick food/bathroom breaks. She'll split the drive between two days so that the cats have a break to get some food, water, and use the litterbox without being in a moving vehicle.

Despite the drugs, Timmy is meowing a lot, and Maceo chimes in every so often. About an hour into the drive, Timmy manages to work the zippers on the round tunnel door open enough to squeeze out, and Maceo soon follows behind him. Sandy considers letting them stay out of the tunnel, since they stopped meowing once they escaped, but in just a few minutes they are crawling on top of her and it's no longer safe to drive. She gets off at the next exit and puts them back into the tunnel. She figures out that if she puts the zippers at the bottom of the round door, Timmy can't use gravity to his advantage and bat at them until they open up enough for him to get out.

The cats settle down and go to sleep a couple hours later and are quiet for the rest of the drive to Santee. They are both awake again when Sandy parks the car at the Hampton Inn. They happily get into their pet carriers since it means they are finally getting out of the car! She sets up their litter box and food dishes in the room, then lets them out of their carriers. Maceo runs around, unphased by his new surroundings. Timmy is a bit more cautious, checking around all the corners to make sure there are no other animals poised to pounce on him.

Once they establish that the coast is clear, they both settle in and chow down on some kibble. Sandy pulls out her quarter pounder and fries that she picked up at the McDonald's drive-thru right beside the hotel. It tastes especially delicious since she didn't make any other food stops today and is *really* hungry. Sandy turns on the TV and watches a rerun of *The Big Bang Theory.* She texts Dom to tell him that they made it safely to the hotel. He texts back that he misses her and the kitties already.

When she wakes up two hours later, the TV and lights are still on, and the cats are sleeping, curled up on either side of her. They were all exhausted from the long drive today. She gets up, brushes her teeth, washes her face, puts on her PJs, and climbs back into bed with the kitties for the night.

Chapter 6

The drive the next day is uneventful. Drugging the cats in the morning was a lot more challenging without Dom there to hold them down, but she eventually got them both dosed. They didn't fuss much at all on the 8-hour drive to Orlando. When they arrive at the townhouse where they are staying, Sandy leaves them in the car while she sets up their food, water, and litter box in the first-floor bedroom. Since the house is big, she thinks it will give them a chance to adjust to their new surroundings without being overwhelmed.

When she lets them out of their carriers, they do their usual cautious exploring and sniffing around the room. She closes the bedroom door so she can bring the rest of her stuff in without worrying about them running out of the house. Once she has the car unpacked, she goes back into the bedroom. The cats race out of the room – no longer wanting to be confined in a small area. "I guess you guys are adjusting fine!" she tells them as they explore the rest of the house. There is an open area that includes the kitchen, dining area and living room, with sliding glass doors that open to the screened lanai and 'splash' pool, which is only about 8 x 8 feet square. She walks out to the pool and dips her hand in the water. It's ice cold! The good news is that there is a heated pool in the community that's only half a mile from the house.

Sandy goes up the stairs to check out the second floor. Tim and Maceo trot up the steps behind her. She is surprised that they are being so brave. The primary bedroom is large, with a king-size bed and a full ensuite bathroom with double sinks. That will work out nicely for her and Dom when he arrives next week. There is another bedroom with twin beds, and the last one has bunk beds. There is another shared bathroom between the two bedrooms. A closet holds a stackable washer and dryer in the hallway.

The cats follow Sandy back downstairs. It's quite pleasant outside this evening, so she goes out to sit on the patio. The cats come out and cautiously sniff the screened perimeter. They all enjoy being outside after being cooped up in the car for two days.

"I'm starving, kitties. I need to get some dinner!" She places an order for fish and chips with Uber Eats at a nearby restaurant, so she doesn't have to leave the cats alone in a strange place yet. She can take her meetings remotely tomorrow, but she must be at the NASA facility to meet with the team on Friday. "Let's give Dominic a call. I'm sure he misses us!"

Sandy lets Dom know that they made it to Orlando and gives him an update on the house and the cats. They chat for a while, and then the Uber driver shows up with her food, so Sandy says goodnight to Dom and eats her dinner.

By 8 PM, Sandy is so tired that she gets into her PJs and decides to read in bed for a while. She must have dozed off quickly, because the next thing she knows it's 12:23 AM and now she's wide awake. Mr. Tim and Maceo are curled up together on the bed beside her. She gets out her phone to check for any messages and texts. Then she remembers that Diane, one of her NASA teammates, mentioned in one of their meetings that there were going to be a couple SpaceX launches from Cape Canaveral this week. She also told her about the Space Coast Launches app, which she loaded on her phone before she left Maryland. She opens the app and is surprised to see that there is a launch scheduled for 1:05 AM – just a few minutes from now. The rocket is SpaceX Falcon 9, which is headed for the moon and carrying the Odysseus lunar lander. The last successful US moon landing was in 1972! This one is unmanned and will reach the moon in 3 days. They are prepping for a manned mission to the moon in 2025.

Sandy puts sweatpants and a sweatshirt over her PJs and walks out the front door, checking that no cats are trying to dart out after her. She looks at Google Maps to make sure she is facing east, which is where Cape Canaveral is with respect to Orlando. Several others from the townhouse complex are waiting outside for the launch.

Soon Sandy can see a glowing orange orb rising through the tree line. It climbs straight up into the sky, and then a few moments later, when the second stage ignites, she sees an explosion into a larger sphere of light that quickly disperses. Then she can see the payload, which is just a small white light now, continue up to its ultimate path toward the moon. She loses sight of it a couple minutes later.

Sandy goes inside and climbs back into bed with the cats. "That was pretty cool!" she tells them. They purr when she pets them, then settle back into sleep.

Chapter 7

The next day is packed with meetings from 8 AM through 6 PM. A couple of them are with teams in Maryland, but the majority are with the NASA team and their partners on the Dragonfly Project. Sandy has been working with them remotely for a couple months and is excited about meeting them in person tomorrow. The relationship always feels closer once you meet someone face to face. She was worried that the cats might still be discombobulated after the long drive and settling into a brand-new place, but they are fine and aren't making much noise in the background during her meetings.

When her last meeting ends at 6:15, a few minutes later than scheduled, Sandy puts on her swimsuit and walks to the community clubhouse, which is about half a mile away. She passes some ghost trees – trees that have died due to rising water levels – along the way. They look very eerie, with the trunks rising out of the water with no foliage. There is no one else at the pool at this hour. Sandy dips her toe in the pool – the water is cold! She decides to start in the hot tub. The water is nice and hot, and the jets put out a good stream of bubbles. It feels amazing after sitting at her laptop in meetings all day. After relaxing her muscles for 15 minutes, she is feeling overheated, so she gets out and gets into the pool. The cold water is a shock to her system, but she read that ending your shower with a cold blast is good for the immune system, so this must be great for ramping up her immunities. Sandy cycles back and forth between the hot tub and the pool two more times, then dries off and walks back to the townhouse. Her body feels very relaxed after spending time in the pool and hot tub.

Her first meeting at Cape Canaveral is at 8 AM, and it's about an hour and a half drive from the townhouse. She doesn't want to be late the first day, so she'll need to leave the house no later than 6 AM. The meetings this month will occur at both the NASA building and at their aerospace partner's building in Orlando. Since the majority of the meetings are in Orlando, it made the most sense to rent a house here.

***

The next morning, Sandy arrives at the NASA complex at 7:30 and checks in with the security guard. He issues her a badge that gives her access to the NASA building they'll be working in. She makes her way to the conference room and is happy to see that Ann and Diane are already there. Ann is an aerospace engineer for NASA, and Diane is a systems engineer there.

"Hi, Ann. Hi, Diane," Sandy says as she shakes each of their hands. "So nice to finally meet you in person!"

"It's great to actually be in the same room together!" Diane says.

"Yes, and I'm glad that we spent so many Teams meetings together. I feel like we already know you!" Ann adds. Sandy nods her head in agreement.

The morning consists of a series of briefings on the project. The first one is given by the Program Director, with a comprehensive view of the program's mission and overall milestones. Then the program managers give an overview and status on each of their pieces of the puzzle. They spend the afternoon touring Cape Canaveral, where they get briefed on all aspects of the launches that take place there regularly.

The day wraps up at 6 PM. "That was a great meeting!" Diane says. "I have a much better understanding of what the different teams are doing."

"I agree!" Sandy tells her. "It's so good to see the big picture and understand our team's importance in the overall success of Dragonfly. I'm proud and excited to be part of it."

"Me too," Ann chimes in. "By the way, Diane and I are going to grab some dinner in Cocoa Beach. Do you want to join us?"

"No, I brought my cats along with me, so I must get back to Orlando to feed them. Thanks for the offer, though!"

"That's really cool that you found a place that allows pets!" Diane says.

"Yes, AirBNB seems to cater to animal lovers and there are a decent number of places available that accept them. For an additional fee, of course! But it's worth it for me...I couldn't stand to be away from them for a month."

"We are going to do a day trip tomorrow to Cassadaga Spiritualist Camp. We're planning to get there around 3 in the afternoon, walk around the town, get dinner at Sinatra's Italian restaurant, then take the Spirits Tour in the evening," Ann says. "Any chance you would like to come along?"

"That sounds interesting," Sandy says. "What is a spiritualist camp?"

"Spiritualists believe that life continues after death, and that the deceased can still communicate with the living," Diane explains. "There are a lot of Mediums who live and work in Cassadaga because the spiritual energy is so high there."

"We tried to go last weekend – they only do the Spirits tour on Saturday nights – but it got cancelled because of rain. The weather looks good for tomorrow," Ann adds.

"I'd like to join you. I believe that a person's spirit continues after death," Sandy replies.

"And Sinatra's is in the Cassadaga Hotel, which is notoriously haunted!" Ann tells her.

"Sounds like a fun trip. I'm in! Where should I meet you tomorrow?"

"Let's meet at the Cassadaga Hotel at 3 PM, and we'll go from there," Diane says. "Glad you can join us!" They exchange mobile phone numbers so they can keep in touch in case anything changes.

Chapter 8

Cassadaga Spiritualist Camp was established in 1894 when George Colby, an associate at the Lily Dale Spiritualist center in New York, discovered the high spiritual energy in this area of central Florida and recommended it to his colleagues, who were searching for a place in the south for a spiritual center. George, whose Native American spirit guide was Seneca, was known for his clairvoyance and healing abilities. In 1992, Cassadaga was added to the National Register of Historic Places. About 50 mediums live and/or work there now.

Diane and Ann are already in the parking lot of the Cassadaga Hotel when Sandy pulls in. When she steps out of the car, she can immediately feel the spiritual energy all around her. She's hoping that she isn't overwhelmed, since she is so sensitive to it. "Hello, you two. How was your drive?"

"Not bad at all," Diane says.

"Not bad for you!" Ann laughs. "I drove and Diane made comments about my driving the whole time. We got behind a few geezers who were taking their good old time, and I got impatient."

"She scared me when she sped around them!" Diane defends herself.

"We'd still be driving if I hadn't got past them. How was your drive, Sandy?"

"It wasn't bad at all. Traffic was moving well the whole way."

"So, do you think all of this is a bunch of hooey? Spiritualism, I mean?" Diane asks.

"Well, I don't usually tell people this, but I've had firsthand experience with spirits, so I don't think it's hooey at all. But I am afraid to tell most people because I don't want them to think I am crazy," Sandy says.

"I've had experiences, too!" Ann says. "I saw a ghost in the house I grew up in, and I heard and experienced things moving around in an apartment that I rented. What have you seen?"

Sandy has had so many experiences with spirits at this point that she doesn't have time to list them all, so she just shares the most personal one. "I inherited the house that my birth mother grew up in, and her spirit was still in the house. I never knew her – I was adopted right after I was born, and she died shortly after that."

"I'm so sorry!" Diane tells her. "I lost my mother when I was very young, so I know how hard that is."

"I am lucky – my adoptive parents are awesome.

I had a great childhood and had no idea who my birth parents were until I got the house, and even then, I had to do a lot of digging to figure out who my biological parents are. My ghost mother gave me a lot of clues so I could figure things out. And I felt like I got to know her a bit as I was working through it. My birth father is still alive, and I have a relationship with him now."

"That is so cool!" Ann remarks. "Is your ghost mom still in your house?"

"No, I think she was able to move on. There hasn't been any more activity in our house for a few years."

"Maybe she wanted to meet you!" Ann says. "As an adult, I mean."

"I guess I am the only one who hasn't had that kind of experience," Diane comments. "I think I am too afraid to be open to it. Is that possible?"

"I think some people are more sensitive to spiritual energy than others, but I also think that things come to you when you are ready," Sandy says.

"Let's check out this cool little town," Ann says. "There are a bunch of shops, a fairy trail, and a labyrinth that I want to see."

"Ooo...fairy trail! Let's go there first," Diane suggests.

The trail is a 0.2-mile loop through a colorful, mystical garden, full of plants, flowers, and tiny houses and figurines. They come across a large blue, green, and purple chair, with pink and yellow wings painted on the chair back. They take turns posing in the chair, which makes them look small and winged. They agree to share all their photos in their group chat. They come across a larger pair of pink, purple, and green wings that they can stand in front of and take a few more pics.

"It's amazing how many things people have left along this trail. I wish I had known to bring something to add to the trail! There's a cool shop, The Forget-Me-Not Factory, in old Ellicott City where I live. It's full of this kind of stuff," Sandy says.

"The Fairy Trail is reported to be a spiritual vortex," Ann tells them.

"What does that mean?" Diane asks.

"It's a place of concentrated spiritual energy," Ann explains. "Some believe that a vortex is a gateway to other dimensions."

"That sounds scary! Look, here's the labyrinth!" Diane says. A labyrinth differs from a maze in that there is only one path to follow in and out. There are no dead ends as in a maze. The girls start at the outer circle, making their way slowly toward the center as they practice walking meditation. The labyrinth is said to be a good way to calm the mind and open yourself up for a psychic reading or spiritual encounter. When they make their way back to the beginning on the outer circle, Ann asks if they feel more at ease and open.

"Yes, but I mostly feel hungry," Sandy says.

"Me too!" Diane agrees. "Are you ready to go to Sinatra's and get some dinner?"

"That sounds perfect," Ann says.

Chapter 9

The Hotel Cassadaga, a two-story yellow stucco building with five archways at the front porch, was built in 1927 as a spiritual sanctuary. People come from all around for readings and healings provided by the mediums, psychics, and healers who practice there.

As Sandy walks through the front door to the hotel, she feels as though she is walking into a wall of psychic energy. She sucks in her breath, and Ann asks her if she is OK.

"Yes, I'm fine, but there is a LOT of spiritual energy here."

"That's why we came!" Ann says. Diane looks a bit alarmed.

An older woman, wearing a colorful headwrap and matching purple dress, approaches them. "It's alright, dearies! The spirits here are benevolent. Those of us who practice in Cassadaga regularly focus on keeping negative energies away."

"Are you a medium?" Ann asks her.

"Yes, I am a medium and a psychic. My name is Martha. Would you like a reading today?"

Ann looks excitedly at Diane and Sandy. They can see that she *really* wants to do it, so they both nod their heads yes, Diane a bit reluctantly.

"We do," Ann says, "but right now we're hungry and want to grab some dinner at Sinatra's. Are you available in about an hour?"

"Yes! Just come and find me in the lobby. I'll find a quiet spot for us to talk," Martha tells them.

The hotel is very eclectic, decorated with 1920s period furniture and tapestries. They enter Sinatra's Ristorante through the doors to the left of the hotel lobby, and it smells delicious. There is a piano bar, literally constructed out of three working pianos, along one wall, and patrons can choose to eat dinner there. No drinks are served at the piano bar. The main bar is across the room, and the surrounding walls by the bar are a beautiful coral color. There are glass chandeliers and other glass wall fixtures that create a romantic glow in the room. The girls opt for a table where they can chat more privately.

"Are you two comfortable with getting a reading? You don't have to do it if not," Ann says.

"I'm nervous, but I want to get one, too," Diane says.

"I've had one before in Ellicott City and it was interesting and helpful for me," Sandy tells them. "I want to do it again."

Their server, Gilberto, asks for their drink preferences and they each order a glass of wine. "What are the pianos used for?" Sandy asks him.

"We have performers every night. Sometimes we have dueling pianos. On Saturday evenings we have piano bar karaoke," he says. "It gets crowded, though, so make sure you come early."

"We have the Spirits Night Tour this evening," Diane tells him. "Have you seen any spirits while working in this hotel?"

Gilberto tells them that there are 40 rooms in the hotel, and that room 22 is notoriously the most haunted. An Irishman named Arthur stayed in that room in the 1930s and died at the hotel. He was fond of cigars and gin, and guests have reported smelling cigar smoke even though smoking hasn't been allowed in the hotel for over 20 years.

"Did you ever see him?" Ann asks.

"No, but I have caught whiffs of cigar several times upstairs. But I have seen two little girls running and playing in the second-floor hallway. I thought they were guests until I scolded them about running and they laughed and disappeared before my eyes."

"Any idea who they are?" Sandy asks.

"I think their names are Sarah and Caitlin. On another occasion I heard them laughing and calling out to each other – I thought they were children staying at the hotel, but there was no one around when I searched the hallways. They seem to like to get up to mischief. Many of our guests have reported seeing the girls and Arthur over the years. Some of them come back year after year in hopes of seeing the spirits again. Have you decided on food, or do you need a few minutes?"

"I think we're ready," Ann tells him. "Thanks for taking the time to talk about the hotel with us!" Ann orders the Ravioli, Sandy gets the Tortellini with vodka sauce, and Diane opts for the Eggplant Parmesan. Their meals are delicious, and the serving sizes are so generous that, despite being famished when they got there, none of them can eat everything on their plates.

When they walk back through the lobby, they find Martha at a secluded table near the hotel gift shop. "How was your meal?" she asks them.

"It was delicious!" Diane says. "But too much to eat."

"Yes, they do a great job at Sinatra's. Very generous portions! So, which of you would like to be read first?" Martha says.

"I'll go," Diane says, afraid that she will lose her nerve if she doesn't get it over with.

Martha instructs Diane to sit down in the chair directly in front of her, then closes her eyes and concentrates for a few moments. "I see you achieving great success in a work endeavor. It involves all three of you. Does that make sense?"

"Actually, it does," Diane says, looking surprised by this early insight. "We all work together on a project team."

"Your project will unlock new information about the universe," Martha adds, "But the big discoveries are a few years away."

"Wow, you're two for two. We work for NASA on Project Dragonfly, which is exploring Saturn's largest moon. It won't be ready to launch until 2027, and it will reach Titan in 2030."

"Is Saturn the planet that has the big rings around it?" Martha asks.

"Yes, it is!" Ann tells her. "Funny enough, the rings around Saturn will appear to disappear in 2025, due to the tilt of the two planets with respect to each other. From Earth, we will be looking directly at the edge of the ring, which is less than 1 mile thick, versus 175,000 miles wide. We can see it best when the width is tilted toward us."

"But they are so pretty!" Martha exclaims. "They won't be gone forever, will they?"

"No, they will come back into view in 2032," Ann says.

"That is very interesting, and you all will find great satisfaction working on this project," Martha tells them. "In the meantime, I have a male presence coming in strongly for you, Diane. His name starts with a 'J'...Jack? He's being quite impatient to communicate with you."

"That's my father...his name was John, but he went by Jack. I lost my mother when I was very young. My father was my best friend until he passed away a few years ago."

"He wants you to know that he loves you and that everything is OK. He is at peace and in no pain, and he's with your mother." Diane starts to cry and nods her head, happy to know this. She misses them both so much and feels encouraged that they will meet again when she moves on from this life.

Martha turns to Sandy. "You are a medium, aren't you?"

"Not exactly – I can't communicate with spirits at will, but they do seem to come to me to get their messages across at times," Sandy admits.

"I can see that your intuition is high – your aura is purple, which represents your middle eye," the Medium continues. "Someone is here for you now. It's your mother. She wants you to know that she was stuck for a long time – harboring ill will toward her sister – but when she finally forgave her, she was able to move on."

Sandy nods her head. "I knew that she was stuck for a while. She was in the house I inherited from her father. I was hoping that she had moved on. I haven't felt or seen her for a while."

"She has gone on to a higher plane, and her relationship with her parents and her sister is healed." Sandy feels a huge sense of relief that her mother is at peace. Martha turns to Ann. "Is there anyone you would like to make contact with?" she asks her.

"Yes. My younger brother disappeared nine years ago – his clothing was found covered in his blood, so we believe that he is dead, but the body was never found. He was only five years old when it happened," Ann says.

Martha sits quietly for a while. Ann is afraid she may have dozed off and is startled when her eyes fly wide open and she shouts, "Your brother is not dead!"

"He's not? Where is he?" Ann gasps.

"I believe he is in Florida – I see palm trees and sunshine. Oh – oh – the vision is fading – it's gone now," Martha says as she slowly shakes her head.

"Andrew is still alive!" Ann says with shock and awe. "Can you tell me anything more?"

"I'm sorry, there's nothing more right now," Martha says. "But he will contact you again when he's ready."

"How???"

"Your mother is his spirit guide," Martha tells her. Now it's Ann's turn to burst into tears. Her mother passed away four years ago, and Ann believes that the stress of losing her son, along with an unhealthy lifestyle, contributed to her early death. Ann's heart is breaking that her brother has been lost and alone for so long, but she is comforted to know that her mother is helping him find his way. And hopeful that she will be reunited with her brother sometime in the future.

When they finish with the reading, they still have about an hour before the Spirits Tour starts, so they decide to do some shopping.

"That was a great reading!" Diane says.

"Yes," Ann agrees. "I feel like she was legit."

"Yeah, she got everything right for me," Sandy adds.

They make their way into the Cassadaga Psychic shop. They find a wide variety of crystals there, along with jewelry, books, and other gifts. It's fun to look at everything, and the crystal stones are beautiful. Ann wishes she could buy them all, but they are a bit pricey. She settles on a small book about crystals, so she can read about each of their healing properties then purchase one or two of the most beneficial ones for herself later. Diane finds a beautiful pack of Tarot cards to buy.

"Look, they have pendulums!" Sandy says. "I like listening to Rachel Dratch's podcast, *Woo Woo*. It's about celebrities' experiences with ghosts and other psychic phenomena. Rachel's partner on the podcast, her longtime friend Irene, has a crystal pendulum that she uses at the end of every show. The guest asks a secret question, and the pendulum gives a yes or no answer based on the direction of its swing. They call it Pengie."

"I love Rachel Dratch! She was so funny on SNL – Debbie Downer was my favorite character," Diane says.

"The pendulum sounds pretty silly to me," Ann says.

"Yes, it does, but Irene picked a whole season of football games correctly in 2014 using the pendulum. And she seems to have a good track record with her guests when 'Pengie' makes a prediction for their personal questions," Sandy tells her. She looks through the array of pendulums, and finally settles on a gorgeous purple, white, and yellow swirled jasper stone. The stone is shaped like a teardrop, with a pointed end, and hangs from a silver chain. The chain is decorated with two sections of tiny stones in purple, maroon, gold, and white hues. "This one is calling to me...I'm going to buy it."

"That one is fabulous. I'm surprised we still have it here...I've seen a lot of customers admiring it since it came in last week," the clerk says as he's ringing up Sandy's purchase.

"It caught my eye immediately," Sandy tells him.

"Jasper is a wonderful stone. It's known for grounding and stability and reminds us that we are here to bring joy to others, not just for the benefit of ourselves."

"I can stand to be reminded of that!" Sandy says.

"I think we all need that lesson from time to time," Diane agrees.

Chapter 10

The Spirits Night Tour starts in a large room at the back of the Cassadaga Spiritualist Camp headquarters. Their spiritual guide for the evening is Jamie, who begins the evening providing a history and background on the spiritualist community. The darkened room has a projector and screen set up in the front, a table with flashlights on a table to the left, and some cat toy balls that are sensitive to vibration at the front of the room. Jamie explains that spirits like to be recognized, and they will make the lights come on when they are seeking attention. If they believe that they are being ignored, they may cause trouble with the projector or other equipment. When one of the flashlights comes on, Jamie quickly says, "I see you. I know you are here!" The light turns itself off. This happens numerous times throughout the presentation. The cat balls light up and turn off periodically as well. Jamie has a computer program that picks up and amplifies electronic voice projections (EVP) created by the spirits in the room. Male and female voices can be clearly heard from the speakers. A female voice says, "Ann, Ann!"

"Did you hear that?" Ann asks Sandy.

"Yes, a woman is calling your name!" Sandy says.

"That sounded just like my mother!"

Another female voice announces, "We are not dead!"

"OK, this is really creeping me out," Diane whispers. Male voices come through from time to time, too, but it's not always easy to decipher what they are saying.

The presentation wraps up, and Jamie leads them all out onto the dark streets of Cassadaga. "Take lots of pictures, and keep your flash on," Jamie tells them. "The light reflects off the electromagnetic waves that the spirits collect and will show up as an orb on your photos."

"How can you tell it's an orb and not just a street or house light?" a tall, older man on the tour asks.

"Take two or three photos in the same spot. A light will be stable in the same place for all shots. An orb will move location or disappear between photos. It will not be in the same spot in two pictures in a row. And just be warned – some of the newer phones correct for the random spots and they won't show up. If you have an old digital camera, that works the best. That's what I'm using."

The tour group, busily snapping photos, slowly walks down Stevens Street. Sandy thinks that she has captured two green orbs near the bushes in front of a home along the way. Jamie explained that green orbs appear near you if you are a healer, or if the spirits are performing healing on you. When Sandy enlarges the photo on her phone, she discovers that what she has actually captured is a pair of cat eyes reflecting back at her. When she looks closer at the bushes, she sees a black cat sitting there, blinking.

"Well, aren't you a little cutie!" Sandy says. He's quite friendly and wanders over to her to be petted.

"I forgot to mention, there is a feral cat community in Cassadaga," Jamie explains. "They are very tame, and there is a group here, *Paws to Help*, that spays, neuters, and feeds the cats. They even do a yearly cat calendar to raise money to support their efforts." Now that it's been brought to their attention, the group is spotting cats all along the way. Sandy wishes that she had purchased a calendar along with her pendulum. The store is now closed for the night.

They arrive at Seneca Park, where the Spirit Pond, which connects to Lake Colby, is located. Jamie leads them to a rock, which is situated between two tall palm trees, in front of the pond. "This spot where I am standing," Jamie explains while standing on the rock, "is the center of a spiritual vortex. The veil between the physical realm and the spiritual dimension is very thin in a vortex. Many orbs are captured in photos at this spot." She has each person stand on the rock, while she takes two photos as baseline shots, then she asks them to stretch out their arms and call in the spirit of someone close to them who has departed, then she takes two additional photos.

Orbs show up in nearly all the photos when the spirits are being called in. Jamie tells them that human spirits typically show up as white orbs, animal spirits are yellow or brown in color, and healers show up as green. By the pond, Sandy doesn't need Jamie to tell her that her mother is there. She can see Maria in more than just orb form. The physical manifestation of her is there for a moment, smiling warmly at Sandy. She blows her a kiss, then disappears. She looks to Jamie to see if she saw her, too, and she nods knowingly at Sandy. Jamie is discreet about this and doesn't mention it to the group...she knows this is a private moment between Sandy and her mother.

As Ann stands in the vortex, Sandy sees an older version of Ann standing beside her. "What does your mother look like?" Sandy asks her when she walks back to where she and Diane are waiting.

"Ann looks just like her mother," Diane says. Diane and Ann have been friends since middle school and spent many days at each other's homes while they were growing up. Ann nods in agreement and asks why Sandy wants to know.

"I saw her standing beside you. She looks just like

you, only older," Sandy tells her. Ann is a beautiful woman, and so is her mother. They share the same bright blue eyes.

Ann's eyes fill with tears. "I could feel her there beside me. She was on my left side, wasn't she?"

"Yes, she was," Sandy confirms.

"Was anybody standing beside me?" Diane asks.

"I didn't see anyone, but I could see the image on Jamie's camera, and there were several orbs around you," Sandy tells her.

"I called in my dad," Diane tells them. "I think I could feel him with me. I really hope it was him."

"Your dad was awesome," Ann says. "He was a good father, and he did it all on his own. Your mom was already gone when I met you in 7th grade. Jack was kind and welcoming to me always."

"He was my best friend," Diane replies. "And he loved all my friends."

The next stop is the Colby Memorial Temple, named in honor of the camp founder, George Colby. The temple hosts church services on Sunday mornings, and healing meditation and message services on Wednesday evenings.

The temple, which was built in 1923, is a large, white Mediterranean style structure. Inside, it looks like a typical church, except instead of religious artifacts such as crucifixes, arks, or scrolls, it is decorated with a sunflower motif. The sunflower represents spiritual growth and enlightenment. Spiritualists believe in the Infinite Intelligence and the continuation of life after death. Many Spiritualists are aligned to other philosophies such as Christianity, Buddhism, and even Agnosticism.

Jamie leads them to the Séance Room, which is located behind the stage where services take place. Séances, conducted to communicate with the spirits of those who have passed on from this life, are held with a maximum of 12 participants, and no video recordings are allowed. However, audio recordings are made for every session. Since this is a sacred space, the tour participants are not allowed to enter the room but are able to look in through the doorway.

"I wish we could have joined the séance that was held this evening," Ann says.

"Me, too!" Sandy agrees.

"I checked the website a week ago," Diane tells them, "And the séance for this evening was already sold out! They only do them three times a month, so with only 12 seats, they sell out fast."

"I definitely want to come back and do it sometime," Ann says.

As the girls go back to their cars to head home for the night, they agree that this was the best ghost tour they have ever been on.

Chapter 11

Sandy heads to the airport to pick up Dominic. He'll be in Florida with her for the week, and she can't wait to see him. Orlando International Airport is packed when she pulls up to the arriving flights pick-up area. Dom looks so handsome standing on the curb...she can't wait to get her hands on him when they get back to the townhouse. She pops open the trunk so he can load his bike, which he checked on the plane in a special shipping case, and his suitcase.

"How was your flight?" Sandy asks Dom.

"It was good. The flight was on time, and except for some rambunctious kids heading to Disney, uneventful."

"That's good! The cats are going to be excited to see you!"

"I can't wait to see the little furballs," he says. Sandy is surprised that he is admitting that he missed them. He usually pretends that he thinks they are a nuisance. She knows deep down that he loves them as much as she does. "But I'm *really* hungry. Can we stop somewhere along the way and get some lunch?"

"Sure – there's a place called *Rock & Brews* that I've been wanting to try. It's near the Margaritaville Hotel in Kissimmee. Supposed to have good food and a nice selection of craft beers."

"Sounds like my kind of place!"

The restaurant has a cool vibe – there's a big guitar neck complete with strings and frets outside, and the inside is decorated with a multitude of band posters and album covers on the walls. There is a continuous stream of classic MTV music videos playing on a large monitor above the bar.

"I like this place!" Sandy says.

"Yeah, and they have Space Dust IPA on draft, so that's an immediate thumbs up from me," Dom agrees.

"This drink, *Stairway to Heaven*, sounds just like the Painkiller that I get in New Smyrna Beach," Sandy says as she points at the drink menu. "I'm getting that! You know it's my favorite."

"Yeah, that's your go-to! You love a Painkiller."

Rock & Brews is known for their craft burgers – Sandy gets the Hamburguesa, which has roasted poblanos, fired jalapeños, and Chihuahua cheese on it, and Dom goes for the Artisan Blue, with blue cheese, applewood bacon, and garlic aioli. The burgers are cooked perfectly – juicy on the inside and a little charred and crispy on the outside. Delicious.

The cats are hiding when Dom and Sandy arrive at the townhouse, but as soon as they hear Dom's voice, they come rushing out to greet him.

"Hello, Mr. Tim! Hey, little Maceo!" He reaches down and swoops them both up in his arms. They lick his face and purr loudly. "Quit licking me! I don't like that," he tells them.

"That means that they accept you as part of their family," Sandy tells him.

"I don't need a bath, cats."

"What *do* you need?" Sandy asks flirtatiously, as she cups his firm butt in her hand.

"I think you already know the answer to that question," he says. Sandy takes his hand and leads him up the stairs to the main bedroom. "Cats, you're not invited. I'll play with you later."

"This room is spacious! And the bed is huge," Dom observes as he falls backward onto the mattress and pulls Sandy down on top of him, then flips her over so that he is on top of her. He gives her a long, lingering kiss on her mouth, then gently bites her right ear, then her left, then moves on to kiss her neck. He knows that this drives her wild, and she is soon wriggling with excitement beneath him, urging him on.

Dom lifts Sandy's shirt over her head, quickly unhooks and tosses her bra aside, and takes her nipples into his mouth, one at a time. He stops for a moment to take off his shirt and strip off his pants and undershorts. Then he comes back to his wife, removing her jeans and panties. He draws a line with his tongue from her chest down her torso. He takes his time kissing the inside of each of her thighs, then buries his face between her legs and laps her up like she's an exquisite delicacy. Sandy moans with pleasure as she grabs and strokes him. He is hard as a rock, and she is begging for him to be inside her. Happy to please, he slowly eases himself into her and Sandy gasps as he sinks in to the hilt. A week is a long time for the two of them to be apart, so it doesn't take long at all for Sandy to climax. Dom is ready to follow, but she makes him stop while she flips them over so that she is on top and can climb off.

Sandy then takes him into her mouth and slowly moves up and down, circling with her tongue. She can tell he is approaching climax, so she slows down and makes him wait. She teases him with several more cycles, then finally brings him over the edge.

"Wow, that was amazing," he gasps. Sandy snuggles in beside him, and they both drift off for a nap. When Sandy wakes up an hour later, Dominic isn't in bed beside her any longer. She hears him downstairs playing with the cats. She rolls over and screams.

"Ann, what are you doing here?" Then Sandy realizes that it isn't Ann at all. It's Ann's mother, a shimmering blond-haired ghost, wearing a blue dress that accentuates her deep blue eyes. She is floating in front of the mirror in the corner. Sandy pulls up the sheet to cover her exposed chest, even though she knows that spirits are not embarrassed or concerned about sex and nudity like the living. They take it in stride.

When Dom hears Sandy's scream and runs up the stairs, Ann's mother disappears. "What's going on?"

"There was a ghost just here," Sandy says.

"Of course there was," Dom replies. He is used to Sandy being a spirit magnet and has come to accept that this will happen from time to time. "What did it want?"

"The ghost is the mother of my friend Ann, who works at NASA. I saw her when I went to Cassadaga with Ann and Diane this past weekend. She must have a message that she wants delivered to Ann, but she's gone now."

"They always come back," Dom tells her.

"Yes, yes they do," Sandy agrees.

Chapter 12

Dom and Sandy are big fans of the Baltimore Orioles baseball team, who have spring training in Sarasota, Florida. They have tickets for today's game against the New York Yankees at Ed Smith Stadium this afternoon. The game is sold out, but they were able to get standing room only tickets. Since the stadium is relatively small and well laid out, they can walk around and see the game easily. They find a spot on the upper deck to the right of home plate and stand at the railing. They have a great view.

By the bottom of the 5th inning, there are no runs scored by either team. "This game is kinda boring," Dom says. "And I'm getting hungry. I'd rather get something other than hot dogs and peanuts to eat. Do you want to leave and go to Gecko's Grill? It's on the way back to the townhouse, and they have good fish there. The game will probably be on in the bar."

"Sure, that sounds good," Sandy says. "I'm getting tired of standing."

As they are walking out, they hear the crowd erupt with cheers and clapping. "Figures! Austin Hayes just hit a homerun," Dom tells Sandy. By the time they get to Gecko's Grill and sit down at the bar, the score for the game is 3-0, Orioles. There was another homerun hit while they were driving that resulted in two more runs for the O's. They watch the rest of the game while enjoying beers and the fresh catch of the day. The Orioles beat the Yankees 7 to 3.

"Guess we should have stayed for the whole game!" Dom remarks.

"Who would have guessed that a no-score game would turn into such an exciting match," Sandy tells him. "The food was definitely better here, though." Dominic nods in agreement.

***

The next week, Dom works remotely from the townhouse, and blocks off his calendar on several days so he can get long workouts in to train for the triathlon in November. He plans to work 25 hours and take 15 hours of vacation to take advantage of the warm weather in Orlando. The Aquatic Center at the National Training Center in Clermont has an outdoor pool with 50-meter swim lanes on certain days, so he can do great lap swim workouts there. He loves swimming outside, and Maryland is too cold for most of the year to keep an outdoor pool heated, but he does enjoy swimming in the outdoor pool at the Pasadena YMCA in the summer.

There are several bike trails in the Orlando area. The West Orange trail is 22 miles long and was converted from railroad tracks that once carried citrus fruit to market. It's now a smooth, nicely paved bike trail. Dom finds that one difficult to ride because it goes through several suburban areas, so there are many stops along the way and places where the trail crosses busy roads. The Van Fleet trail, another converted rails-to-trails route, is much more rural and 29 miles long. Dom prefers that one and plans to ride it a couple more times while he's in Orlando.

Sandy has on-site meetings all week with her project team at the Lockheed Martin facility in Orlando. Diane and Ann both live close to NASA and have over an hour drive to the facility, so she invited them to stay at the townhouse, since they have extra bedrooms. They happily took her up on the offer and will be staying with her and Dom after work this evening.

Chapter 13

A blond-haired, blue-eyed boy is crying in the corner of an attic. It's dark, he's scared, and feeling very alone. The rain is making a loud racket on the roof and running down the windows so fast that he can barely see out. The streetlamps in the distance throw a stingy dim light, but otherwise, the darkness outside is nearly as black as inside.

He cringes as he hears footsteps on the attic stairs. The mean woman enters the room. She's dressed in a plaid flannel shirt and blue jeans, and has her gray hair pulled back into a ponytail. She looks as old as his granny. "Johnny, if you behave, I will let you have a lamp up here."

"My name is Andrew!" he shouts at her.

"Your name is Johnny now. I don't want you to say your name is Andrew ever again or you will be locked in this attic forever. I need to trust you not to try to run away again."

"I'm hungry," he whimpers.

"Are you going to behave?" Andrew nods his head yes. "I'll bring you some supper and a lamp," she says. She leaves the room, locks the door from the outside, and

walks downstairs. When she comes back, she plugs in the lamp and places a bowl of beef stew and a glass of water on a small table to the left of the cot where he slept last night.

"Thank you, ma'am," he says, and hungrily digs into the stew. It's the best tasting food he's ever had, probably because he hasn't eaten in over a day.

"Don't call me ma'am! Call me Nana. Remember, I am your grandmother and I'm taking care of you now because your mother is dead." She goes back down the steps and leaves him alone in the attic once again.

Andrew knows his mother isn't dead and that this woman isn't his granny, but he has no choice but to nod his head yes if he doesn't want to starve to death. He can hear crying through the floorboards and Nana's voice talking to someone. There must be another kid locked up downstairs. He can't make out what she is saying, but she sounds angry, like she is threatening them.

Sandy wakes up from her dream and looks at her watch. It's nearly time for her alarm to go off, so she gets out of bed and goes down to the kitchen to make some coffee for her guests. Ann comes down a few minutes later.

"That coffee smells delicious!" Ann says.

Sandy grabs two mugs out of the cupboard and hands one to Ann. "Help yourself! Sugar and cream are on the counter. And there's some coconut milk if you prefer non-dairy."

"Great, thanks! I had a very vivid dream about Andrew last night," Ann tells her.

Sandy's jaw drops open. "I think I dreamt about Andrew last night too! Blond hair, blue eyes. He was locked in an attic."

Now it's Ann's turn to be surprised. "I think we had the same dream! A woman was trying to convince him that his name was Johnny, and she was his grandmother. This was a scene from the past, though, because Andrew looked like he did when he disappeared nine years ago. He would be bigger now."

"Yes, we had the same dream. He was a young boy in my dream. Someone is trying to get a message to us," Sandy says.

"What should we do?"

"I didn't get too many details in my dream. What exactly did you see?" Sandy asks. Diane comes down the stairs just in time to hear the last bit.

"Who saw what last night?" Diane asks. Ann describes her dream in as much detail as possible, and Sandy says it is pretty much identical to her dream.

"I think we need to wait for more information," Sandy tells them. "Someone is trying to help us find Andrew. We need to be patient."

"Not one of my virtues!" Ann admits.

"Patience is hard for all of us," Diane says. "But

both of you having the same dream has to mean something."

Dom walks into the kitchen. "Uh oh. Sandy and her dreams have gotten her into trouble. Now she has you dreaming, too?" he teases Ann.

The three of them get ready for work and head off to the facility for a long day of meetings. Dom sets his laptop up on the kitchen table and logs into his work network.

Ann has trouble concentrating in the meeting because she is thinking about her brother. If only they had a few more clues! She realizes that she hasn't heard what the presenter has said for the last fifteen minutes. Thankfully, no questions came her way, or she would have had to admit that she wasn't paying attention. She gets up and gets herself another cup of coffee, hoping that the caffeine will make it easier to focus on work instead of obsessing over Andrew.

Chapter 14

The team has already put in 50 hours of work for the week by Friday, so the project leaders are giving everybody half a day off. Sandy, Diane, and Ann decide to spend the afternoon at ICON Park in Orlando. Admission and parking are free, unlike many of the other parks in Orlando, which are becoming more and more expensive. They like the idea of just paying for the attractions that they want to do and it's the perfect day for an outing - sunny, 75 degrees, and a little breezy. Dom has a long bike ride planned for the trail, so he doesn't mind Sandy hanging out with the girls.

"I want to do The Wheel!" Diane says as soon as they enter the park and see the 400-foot-tall Ferris wheel.

"OK, I'm game," Ann agrees.

"I'm not thrilled with heights," Sandy says, "but it says you are allowed to take beverages that you buy at the Wheelhouse Bar onto the ride. I'll be fine if I drink some liquid courage." Diane and Ann think that's a great idea, so they make their way up to the bar. The bartender brings them their fruity drinks and confirms that they can carry them on the wheel.

The glass pods are large, but the park isn't that crowded this afternoon, so they get a compartment to themselves. There are Bluetooth speakers in the pods that you can connect to your phone, so Sandy gets Spotify going and queues up requests from Ann and Diane. Diane starts dancing and gets the other two to join in.

The wheel slowly rotates, and the view gets increasingly better as their pod nears the top. "This is amazing!" Sandy says.

"Yes, you can see all of Orlando from up here!" Ann chimes in.

"Not scared of the height?" Diane asks.

"I'm fine as long as I don't look straight down!" Sandy tells her.

When they get back to the loading platform at the bottom, they try to bribe the operator to let them stay on for another round.

"We're not allowed to do that," he tells them nicely, even though he is probably asked this question a hundred times a day. "But if you go out and get another ticket, you can get back on quickly, since there is no line today."

They haven't had lunch yet, so they decide that they'd rather eat than take another spin on the wheel. There are several restaurants that look great at the park, and Ann really wants to try Sugar

Factory. The place is cute and candy themed, with lots of delicious drinks, milkshakes, and desserts, along with hearty meals.

"Those onion rings look amazing," Sandy says. "If I get those as an appetizer, would you eat some?" Diane and Ann vigorously nod their agreement.

The onion rings are delicious. Diane gets the buffalo chicken sandwich, Ann gets the Belgian waffle, and Sandy gets the grilled cheese sandwich. Everything is yummy.

One of the walls is covered with pink silk roses and has fuchsia neon lights that spell out 'Hey there wild thing.' "We need to get a pic in front of that sign," Sandy says, so they ask their server to take a photo as they pose in front of it.

"I'd like to go to Madame Tussauds wax museum," Sandy says. "I've never been to one and I hear that the wax statues are very realistic. That'll be a good place to walk around."

"Yes, I've been to one in London," Ann tells them. "I liked it a lot and wouldn't mind going to this one."

"I'm in," Diane says.

The first clue that the museum is going to be good is that Diane bumps into the likeness of Vin Diesel near the entrance to Madame Tussauds and says, "Excuse me!" before she realizes that he isn't a real man. Sandy and Ann laugh so hard that everyone in line for the museum turns to look at them to see what all the fuss is about.

Abraham Lincoln sits in a chair in a black suit and bowtie, though he isn't wearing his trademark top hat. Ann sits in the chair beside him and poses with her hand on his arm. She poses with Apollo 11 astronaut Neil Armstrong next. Ann and Diane pose together with Martin Luther King, and Sandy gets Diane to take a pic of her posing with Albert Einstein. They are amazed at how lifelike the wax mannequins are.

They continue through the museum and see Taylor Swift, Andy Warhol, Katie Perry, Michael Jackson, Marilyn Monroe, Jimmy Fallon, Johnny Depp, and many others. All the likenesses are beautiful works of art. They each take a photo sitting on a bike with E.T. in the basket in front of them and the full moon shining from behind.

As they are rounding the corner near the museum exit, Ann does a double take. Sandy notices the startled look on her face and asks what's wrong.

"I could have sworn that I just saw my mother standing right there, but there is no one there now."

"There's a piece of paper lying on the floor right there," Diane says as she walks over to pick it up. She hands it to Ann.

"You are going to think I'm crazy, but this smells like the fragrance that my mother always wore," Ann says. She unfolds the paper and sees the image of a Mediterranean Revival style mansion with curved, red-clay roof tiles, and arched windows and doorways. "This has to be another clue."

"I think you're right," Sandy agrees. "Do you know where there are houses like this around here?"

"That style is very popular in Florida," Diane says. "But it would have to be a pretty exclusive neighborhood. That is not an inexpensive home."

"There's no house number or street marking in this picture," Ann says. "This is so frustrating!"

"We just need to keep our eyes, ears, and minds open for more signs," Sandy reassures her. "Your mom is obviously trying to help us."

Chapter 15

Being away from the office has taken a toll on Sandy's work in the Maryland office, so she spends Saturday morning catching up on requests and emails from her colleagues at APL. Dominic has work to catch up on, too, and he will fly back to Baltimore Sunday afternoon, so he wants to do some fun things with Sandy this afternoon and tomorrow before he heads home.

"What do you want to do this afternoon?" Dom asks her.

"I'm hungry for Thai food. There's a good restaurant, Thai Café, just a couple blocks from Lake Eola. It's such a pretty day that we could go for a walk around the lake after we have lunch."

"That sounds good. Are you almost finished working?"

"Yeah. I have a report I want to finish, then I'm done. Should take me about 30 more minutes."

Dominic drives them downtown, and they luck out and find a parking spot on Magnolia Street right in front of Thai Café. Dominic orders his usual, basil fried rice with shrimp, and Sandy gets her favorite, chicken in Thai basil sauce. She even splurges on a Thai iced tea. The food comes out fast and is loaded with fresh vegetables and served at the perfect level of spiciness – hot, but not so spicy that it overpowers the other flavors in the dish.

They finish up their meals and walk three blocks to Lake Eola. It's a beautiful, clear day, with just a few clouds in the sky. This time of the year is wonderful in Orlando because it is warm, in the mid-70s, with no humidity. The 0.9-mile loop around the lake is teeming with people, dogs on leashes, and wild birds. In the center of the lake, a beautiful green fountain pours water over two layers of curved surfaces, then shoots several streams from the circumference around the top. A 75-foot stream erupts from the center of the circle of smaller fountains. The fountain looks gorgeous with the sunlight sparkling off the water.

"There are reports of a brown terrier who haunts this lake," Sandy tells Dominic.

"I see a lot of dogs here. How can you tell if they are ghosts?"

"For one thing, a ghost dog is probably not on a leash," Sandy laughs. "People report seeing a little brown dog that is there one minute and disappears the next."

As they walk around the lake, they see a congregation of white egrets sitting in the shade under a tree. No signs of the ghost dog, though. At the far side of the lake, a bevy of white swans with long, elegant necks is swimming gracefully across the water.

"Oh, look!" Dom says. "There are three black swans over there. I never saw a black swan in real life."

"Wow! Me neither. They are so pretty! That one right there is huge!"

"Hey, there is one with a black head and a white body! He looks weird."

"No body shaming!" Sandy tells him.

"I accept swans of all colors," Dominic assures her, "I just was surprised by his unusual coloring."

Toward the end of their loop around Lake Eola, they come upon a large sculpture called the Muse of Discovery. The 40-foot-long sculpture of a woman lying on her belly is constructed of limestone and earth and was created by Meg White of Kentucky.

"Wasn't Meg White the drummer for the White Stripes?" Dominic asks.

"Yes, but not the same Meg White. The sculptor is from Kentucky, the drummer is from Detroit."

The Muse's head, arms and leg stick out above the grass, and the rest of her body is buried beneath the earth. Legend has it that if you sit in her open palm, she will whisper your hidden potential to you. Visitors are welcome to climb and sit upon the interactive sculpture, so Dominic decides to try his luck and sit in her hand. Sandy gets an alarmed look on her face as he sits down.

"What's the matter? The sign says you're allowed to climb on her," Dom says.

"No, it's not that. Ann's mom is standing right beside you."

"The ghost?"

"Yes."

"Dom looks over to the left where Sandy is pointing. "Is she still there?"

"Yes, and she's pointing at the ground," Sandy says. Dominic looks down and sees a round disk that looks like a coaster you put under a glass. He picks it up and carries it over to Sandy. Sandy wipes the dirt off it and sees that it's a Christmas ornament, and it says 'Howey-in-the-Hills'. When she looks up at the sculpture, she sees that Ann's mother is gone. "This has to be another clue."

Sandy is worried that if she digs into this right now, she will be drawn into solving the mystery and won't be able to focus her attention on Dominic, so she decides to wait until he leaves tomorrow to tell Ann what happened. She is going to be in Florida for two more weeks and won't see Dom again until she drives back to Maryland. He has been very patient with her ghost hunting adventures, but she doesn't want to push it.

Chapter 16

"What do you want to do on your last day in Orlando?" Sandy asks Dominic. Timmy meows and Maceo winds himself around Dom's legs as if to say, 'Play with us!'

"I am going to miss these two little vermin," Dominic tells her, as he picks a cat up in each of his arms. Maceo licks Dom's nose, and Timmy rubs his head against his hand. "How about Disney Springs?"

"I thought you said the Disney parks are too expensive," Sandy says.

"It's not a park. There are restaurants and shops, parking is free, and there is no admission fee. Some of the restaurants look pretty good."

"OK, sounds like fun."

As Dom promised, there is lots of free parking in the parking garages nearby. They park in the Lime garage and follow the overhead signs showing the number of open spots on each level. Green lights above the spots show open spaces. They park and take the escalators down to the main level, where they line up to go through a metal detector, then take the escalators down to the main entrance.

"This is so pretty!" Sandy says. Disney Springs is nicely laid out, with bridges crossing over blue water, lots of trees and flowers, and four nicely designed 'neighborhoods.' First, they enter the Town Center, with attractive white stucco storefronts, pretty fountains, and a variety of dining venues. They walk on to the Landing, which provides gorgeous views of the water and is home to many upscale restaurants.

As they walk past The Edison, Sandy spots, in the entryway to the restaurant, a gorgeous 10-foot-tall industrial clock with exposed gears beautifully lit with multicolored lights. "I want to eat here!" Sandy shouts to Dominic, who is walking away toward the next restaurant.

"You are such a nerd!" he laughs. The restaurant is decorated to look like a steam-punk themed 1920s electric company.

"Thank you! Nerds rule the world," Sandy tells him. She makes him take a photo of her posing in front of the clock.

"The menu looks good, so it works for me," Dom says.

The restaurant is full of old stuff, including a red steam engine, a large antique scale, and huge boiler room doors decorating a brick wall. In addition to having a totally cool vibe, The Edison has a top-notch menu. They start with the

Monumental Pretzel, and when it comes out, it truly is enormous. It comes with two yummy dips – pimento cheese and honey mustard.

Sandy has the Patented Old Fashioned, and Dom orders Bourbon on a big rock. Since the pretzel is so big, they decide to share an entrée, and opt for the Tomato Soup and Gooey Grilled Cheese Sandwich. Good thing they are sharing because it is also a big serving.

"That was delicious and now I am so full!" Sandy complains. "Let's walk over to the Marketplace and work off some of this food."

There is a line of people waiting to get in to one of the stores. "What's going on over here?" Dom asks Sandy.

"It's the Lego store. Wow, that line is crazy!"

"Look, there are sculptures around the outside of the building. Let's look at those." There is a 15-foot-long green Loch Ness monster, constructed with Lego blocks, in the lake beside the store. "How many pieces do you think are in this one?"

One of the employees standing outside overhears him and tells them that there are over 120,000 Lego bricks in the structure. At the side of the building, there are sculptures of Anna, Elsa, and Olaf from the Frozen animated movie. Chewbacca, Rey, Kylo Ren, Captain Phasma, and a red Stormtrooper of Star Wars fame reside on the other side – large as life and completely constructed of toy bricks. Inside the store, a sculpture of Spiderman is hanging from a doorway, but there are so many people crowded around that they don't even attempt to get closer.

There are a few people gathered on the sidewalks and looking up at the sky. "Oh, I forgot that there is a rocket launch this evening!" Sandy says.

"Do you think we'll be able to see it from here?" Dom asks her.

"The sun is pretty bright, but there may be just enough cloud cover that we will be able to get a glimpse of it," Sandy tells him.

A few minutes later, they can see the vapor plume rising straight up, and when the rocket goes behind a gray cloud, they can see the red flames shining through. Once it clears the cloud, they can't see it anymore, but the vapor trail continues going up.

They wander around the other shops and stop in Goofy's Candy Company, where Sandy buys some chocolate covered coconut patties that are shaped like Mickey Mouse's head. She also wanders into the Christmas Shop and buys a Disney Springs ornament to commemorate their trip. After that, they decide to head back home so Dominic can pack up for his flight back to Baltimore.

"We didn't spend any money, except for lunch, which was totally worth it," Dominic proudly reports as they leave Disney Springs.

"And my souvenirs," Sandy laughs.

Chapter 17

Dom is back in Ellicott City, and Sandy is working at NASA again today. The drive wasn't too bad this morning since she left at the crack of dawn. This got her into the facility before 7 AM, and their meetings don't start until 8, so she has time to work on her laptop for an hour. Sandy hopes that Ann gets in a little early so she can tell her about seeing her mom at Lake Eola and show her the ornament that Dom found.

Fortunately, Ann is an early bird, too, and gets there before anyone else is around. "I need to tell you something," Sandy excitedly tells Ann.

"What's up?" Ann replies, looking a bit concerned. "Is something wrong with the project?"

"No, nothing like that. It's about your mom. What's her name, by the way? I don't want to keep calling her ghost mom."

"It's Joan," Ann tells her. "Why, did you see her again?"

"Yes! Dom and I went to Lake Eola for a walk. Do you know where the large sculpture of the woman, The Muse of Discovery, is?"

"Yep, I love that sculpture."

"Dom was sitting in the sculpture's open palm, and Joan appeared right beside him. And she was pointing to this on the ground." Sandy pulls the ornament out of her pocket and shows it to Ann. "I think it's another clue."

"Oh, wow. Howey-in-the-Hills. I know where that is!" Ann tells her.

Diane and several more people roll into the room. "Know where what is?" Diane asks.

"We'll catch you up at lunch time. Sandy found another clue." Ann says.

"Cool beans! Now I am dying to know!!"

Everyone settles in their seats in the conference room, and the Principal Investigator for Dragonfly welcomes everyone to the meeting.

"I have great news this morning. Funding has been approved for the final design phase, construction, and testing for our spacecraft and instrumentation," she tells them. The room erupts with clapping and cheering. Everyone has been nervous with the tight economic environment and political uncertainty this year, so it's a huge relief that they will have the opportunity to continue to work on this important research that they love. "And we have confirmed launch readiness for July 2028." Another round of applause and cheers follows.

Progress updates are made by the various team leads, and then they break off into groups and continue working on their various aspects of the project. The morning goes by quickly, and when lunch is served, Ann, Diane and Sandy grab their sandwiches and head outside to continue the discussion from earlier. Most scientists are open-minded, but they may find the topic of ghosts and spirits a bit off-putting. Men seem especially reluctant, even if they believe in things beyond this world, to admit it.

"I've been anxious all morning to hear what's going on," Diane tells them as they sit down at a picnic table under the trees. Even though it's over 80 degrees and humid today, they feel comfortable in the shade and are happy to warm up a bit after sitting in the cold conference rooms all morning.

"We got another clue," Ann tells Diane. "Sandy saw my mom at Lake Eola and found this ornament where she was standing."

"Well, Dom actually found it," Sandy corrects her.

"Joan was at the lake? Aw, I miss her. She was such a feisty lady. I loved hanging out at your house when we were young," Diane says. "She was a cool mom."

"Yeah, she didn't take any crap off anyone!" Ann replies. "I wish I was more like her!"

"You are like her! You look just like her, and you are a strong woman, too," Diane says. "Howey-in-the-

Hills...is that the clue?"

"I think we need to go there," Ann says. "I know she's trying to help me find Andrew. Howey-in-the-Hills is a town northwest of Orlando. About a 90-minute drive from here."

"The project schedule has us meeting in Orlando again on Friday," Sandy says. "We can go there after we finish working and you can spend the night at my place Thursday, and Friday, too, if it gets too late. Dominic is back in Baltimore, so I would love the company."

"That sounds like a plan," Ann says, and Diane nods.

Sandy doesn't get back to the townhouse until after 7 that night. Timmy and Maceo are waiting at the door for her, and almost trip her as they wind around her legs as she tries to make her way into the kitchen to feed them.

"Sorry I was away so long, babies!" Sandy says. "I know you were getting used to Dominic working from home last week. Only a couple more weeks, and we'll head back home." They chow down greedily on their food while Sandy reheats some leftover shrimp fried rice.

When she sits down on the couch to eat her dinner, they both jump up and settle on either side of her. She finishes her leftovers, then gets out their favorite feathers on a stick toy. They take turns batting at it and chasing it, then Timmy grabs the feathered end in his mouth and proudly trots away with it, as if proclaiming victory. Maceo follows along after him.

Sandy is worn out from the long day, so she stretches out on the sofa and turns on the TV. In no time, she is dozing with Maceo on her belly and Mr. Tim on her legs.

Andrew is struggling to remember his old life. He's been here with his new Nana for 5 years. He knows that because he was 5 when he came here, and on his last birthday, there were 10 candles in his cake. He can still remember his mother's face, though. She was beautiful with blond hair and bright blue eyes. And he remembers his sister, Ann, who had the same color hair and eyes as his mama. Nana spanks him and locks him in the attic anytime he talks about his mama or his sister. When his friends ask him why he lives with his grandmother, he does as Nana told him and says that his mother died in a car crash. He doesn't really believe this, though. Sometimes he can feel his mama reaching out to him – he knows she is still searching for him, and it makes him sad to be away from her. He can see her in his dreams, and she is crying for him. When he cries and tells Nana he misses his mama and his sister, she tells him they are dead and there is no use being stuck in the past. She threatens that if he doesn't shape up, she'll give him something to really cry about.

Once he told Nana that he heard crying from a room below the attic, and she told him he was crazy and beat him so hard that he had black and blue bruises all over his back and bottom. He thought about showing the marks to his teacher at school, but worried that they would tell Nana and then he would be in even more trouble. Things have been going more smoothly lately, since Andrew has been following directions and not asking questions.

When Andrew told Nana that he missed his orange tabby cat, Freddie, she brought home a fluffy, orange-striped kitten. He asked her if he could name it Freddie, and she said he could call it whatever he wants.   The old Freddie's full name was Freddie Krueger Fluffovich, because of his fluffy fur and dagger claws. Andrew doesn't think Nana would appreciate that name, so he secretly names the kitten Freddie Krueger Fluffovich, II, but just calls him Freddie in front of her. Freddie the kitten is very fluffy, too, and he purrs a lot. Andrew has had him about a month now, and he loves him just as much as he loved Freddie the first.

Today, Nana tells him that he has been a good boy, so she is going to take him out for dinner at JB Boondocks restaurant. Andrew loves the fish, chips, and hushpuppies there, so it's always a treat when they go. They usually get a table by the water, so they can watch the boats motor up and down Little Lake Harris. Nana's son, who Andrew must call Uncle Ernie, has a fishing boat, and after they finish their lunch, he is going to take them for a boat ride. He takes them out on the boat often when the weather is nice.

Chapter 18

Ann and Diane arrive at Sandy's townhouse a bit after seven Thursday evening. She shows them to the rooms upstairs where they will be sleeping then they settle down in the family room to chat and enjoy a glass of wine.

"I just remembered my dream from last night," Sandy says. "Andrew was in it."

"What happened?" Ann asks excitedly.

"I was seeing things through Andrew's eyes," Sandy tells her. "He was trying hard to remember what you and your mom looked like. He just celebrated his 10th birthday, so it must have happened about four years ago."

"Oh no! Poor Andrew. He was so small when he was taken. No wonder he can barely remember!" Ann says.

"He was such a sweet kid," Diane says, "Is a sweet kid!" She quickly corrects herself.

"The good thing is that I saw him at a restaurant – JB Boondocks. Do you know where that is?"

"I've been there before!" Ann says. "They have

great fish and chips."

"That's what Andrew said is his favorite!" Sandy says. "Also, he said the name of Nana's son. He calls him Uncle Ernie, and said he takes him out on his boat."

"Who is Nana?" Diane asks.

"The woman who kidnapped him," Sandy says. "She makes him call her Nana and tell everyone that his mother died so now his grandmother takes care of him."

"We need to go there tomorrow after work," Ann says. "Someone at the restaurant might have seen Andrew or know Uncle Ernie."

"I agree, but we need to be careful. Nana and Uncle Ernie could be dangerous if they know we are onto them," Sandy cautions them.

***

The next morning at work drags because the girls are so anxious to get to Howey-in-the-Hills that afternoon. None of them slept well the night before, which isn't helping them focus on work. One of the engineers is droning on about the technical minutia of his project and putting up barely legible charts and graphs detailing every step of his data analysis.

"Someone needs to send this guy to a class on presenting at a high level. He is giving too much detail and not telling us his conclusions and how to apply them to the project," Diane whispers, a little too loudly, to Ann. Ann shushes her, but nods her head in agreement. After an hour, he finally finishes, and no one in the room knows what point he was trying to make.

The day was supposed to wrap up at noon, but they are behind schedule and don't end up finishing until almost one. Everyone is grumbling because they are hungry, and lunch wasn't served today since it was a half day. Ann and Diane jump into Sandy's car, and they take off for Howey-in-the-Hills. In line with how the rest of the day is going, traffic is bad this afternoon, so what should be a 45-minute drive turns into over an hour.

They finally arrive at JB Boondocks and get a table on the deck out back. "I'm starving!" Sandy says. "Let's start with a couple appetizers so we get something quick to nosh on."

"Perfect," Diane says.

"I really like the fish dip here," Ann says.

"OK, let's get that, and how about the Swamp Bites?" Sandy asks. "I always wanted to try alligator."

"Sure, I'm game," Diane says.

"Just tastes like dark meat chicken to me," Ann says, "But I'll eat some." The server comes over to their table and takes their drink and appetizer orders.

"The view is amazing out here!" Sandy observes. "The lake is so pretty!"

"Yeah, I always request an outside table," Ann tells them. "So, how do you think we should ask about Andrew?"

"We don't want to raise suspicions...we need to act casually about it," Sandy says.

"I'm not a good actress. My emotions are easy to read on my face! I am going to keep my mouth shut and my head down," Diane promises.

"I think I can be casual," Ann says.

Their server, Jane, comes back with their drinks and appetizers. "Are you ready to order your meals, or do you need a few more minutes?"

"I think we're ready," Diane tells her. They put in their meal orders.

Before Jane leaves the table, Ann says, "I lost touch with a friend of mine, Ernie, who likes to eat here. He would have come with an older woman and a young boy named Johnny. Do you know them?" Diane looks abruptly down at her appetizers and starts scooping them onto her plate and eating them.

"A lot of people come through here, and I usually don't remember their names. What does he look like?" Ann panics as she realizes that she has no idea what Ernie looks like. She looks at Sandy, who shakes her head no, because she did not see 'Uncle

Ernie' in her dream.

"Ernie is probably in his late 40's/early 50's," Ann ad libs. "He has a boat that he likes to take out on this lake. Johnny has blond hair and blue eyes. Really cute kid. I have a photo of him, but it's about nine years old." Ann opens the photo app on her phone and shows Jane a picture of Andrew.

"Sorry, I don't recognize the boy. A lot of people have boats in these parts."

"No problem. Thanks anyway!"

Diane wasn't lying about not having a poker face. The look of disappointment is clearly on display.

"If we drive around for a while after dinner, maybe I can find the house that was in the picture that your mom left in the wax museum," Sandy suggests.

"That's as good a plan as any," Ann agrees.

Their meals come out fast – Diane and Sandy get the fish fry platter with corn fritters and cole slaw, and Ann gets the Cajun mahi with rice and veggies.

"These fish portions are enormous!" Sandy says. "It's really good!"

"Glad you like it," Ann replies. "Mine is yummy, too."

The portions are so large that they get to-go boxes and take half of their meals with them. They drive around the area near JBs, looking for houses that look like the picture that Ann brought along from the museum. They see a lot of Mediterranean Revival style homes, but none as large or exactly like the one on the paper. After forty-five minutes of driving around in circles, they've had enough and decide to go back to Sandy's house for the evening.

Chapter 19

Timmy and Maceo sprint to the door when they hear Sandy, Diane, and Ann come in.

"You guys are hungry, aren't you?" Sandy says, as she notices their empty bowls. She gives them their favorite kibble and adds water to their fountain.

"They are so cute!" Diane says. She pets Maceo, but he is too busy gobbling down his food to notice.

"What's that water thing?" Ann asks. "Do they like to drink out of it?" The fountain dispenses water from a daisy on top.

"Yes, they love it! It has a filter in it, and the water continually circulates, so it always tastes fresh and cold. It encourages them to drink more, which is good for them," Sandy explains. "I clean it and change the filter once a month." As if on cue, Mr. Tim walks over to the fountain and starts lapping water off the daisy.

"I'm disappointed that we didn't get any closer in finding Andrew," Ann says. "How do we get more guidance?"

"What about that pendulum thing you got

in Cassadaga?" Diane suggests. "Can we ask it questions to get us closer to him?"

"Sure, I'll go get it." Sandy comes back from her bedroom a few minutes later with the pendulum. "I did some research and found out that you are supposed to ask your pendulum what means yes and what means no. Let's start with that."

Sandy holds the pendulum by the chain then says, "Pendulum, show me what 'yes' looks like." The pendulum starts swinging forward and back, away from Sandy, then toward her. "Thank you!" Sandy uses her other hand to stop the pendulum's motion. "Can you show me again what 'yes' looks like?" Once again, the pendulum swings forward and back, even more vigorously this time.

"Well, it's sure about that!" Ann says.

"Now show me what 'no' looks like," Sandy tells the pendulum. This time, the pendulum swings from left to right. "Thank you. Please show me 'no' one more time." The pendulum swings left and right again.

"OK, I think we know this pendulum's code," Diane remarks. "Can I ask the first question?"

"Go for it," Sandy tells her.

"Is Andrew living in Howey-in-the-Hills?" Diane asks. The pendulum vigorously swings forward and back. "That's a yes!"

Ann then asks, "Is my brother in danger?" The

pendulum swings from left to right. Ann breathes a sigh of relief.

"It's hard to ask specific questions when you have to frame them as yes or no," Diane complains.

"Is Andrew within five miles of JB Boondocks restaurant?" Ann asks. The pendulum swings erratically in a circle. "What does that mean?"

"I think it means maybe? Or uncertain?" Sandy suggests.

"Are we going to find Andrew?" Diane asks the pendulum. The pendulum swings strongly forward and back. "Yes! So, we just need to be patient and alert. Sandy, why don't you go back to bed and see if you have any more dreams," Diane teases.

"I don't want to be patient! I miss him so badly that my chest physically hurts me," Ann says, as tears slide down her face.

Diane wraps her arms around Ann and hugs her tightly. "I know sweetie – I'm so sorry. But we're going to find him. Pengie says so!"

"Maybe we should go back to Cassadaga? See if a Medium can reach Joan?"

"That's a good idea," Ann says. "Or maybe even sit in a séance? On the tour, they said that the spiritual energy is particularly strong in that room."

Sandy pulls out her laptop and does a search for

Cassadaga Spiritualist Camp. She finds the events page and tells them that there is a Saturday night séance tomorrow evening. "There probably aren't any spots left this late," Diane says.

"This must be our lucky day," Sandy says. "There are exactly three seats left at the table! Should I book it?"

"Yes!" Ann and Diane shout in unison.

"OK, three seats are booked for the séance tomorrow night at 7 PM!"

***

The next day, Sandy, Ann, and Diane decide to relax at the community pool once it warms up enough. The sky is a clear blue, with only a few wispy clouds scattered about. The forecast for today is sunny with a chance of rain later in the day. As they are walking by a retention pond on the way to the clubhouse, they come upon a family of herons.

"Look, there's a Mama, Papa, and two baby birds over there!" Ann says and points toward the pond.

"Yes, those are Sandhill Cranes. Aren't they pretty? They've been wandering around the neighborhood since we got here a few weeks ago," Sandy tells them.

"Aw, the babies are so cute! But they are brown, not blue," Diane says.

"They get more colorful when they grow up. The

brown helps them hide better," Ann says.

No one is at the pool when they arrive, so they grab three lounge chairs with easy access to the pool and the hot tub. The sun feels wonderful on their skin. "Do you mind if I get my book out? I love to read while sitting by the pool or on the beach," Diane asks.

"That's my favorite thing to do, too!" Sandy replies. "Read away! I brought my Kindle along." Sandy gets her Kindle out of her bag, Ann grabs her book, and they all happily bask in the beautiful day while they enjoy their books in companionable silence.

After half an hour of sunning, Sandy says she is hot, so they decide to take a dip in the pool. The water is cool enough to be refreshing but not shockingly cold. After a few minutes in the pool, they switch to the hot tub, enjoying the massaging action of the bubbles and the relaxing effect of the hot water on their muscles.

"What do you think about having dinner at Sinatra's before the séance?" Ann suggests.

"That's a great idea!" Sandy agrees.

"Yeah, that was delicious last time. I vote yes!" Diane chimes in.

Chapter 20

The sky decided to open wide on Saturday evening, and the rain is pouring down when the girls arrive at the Hotel Cassadaga. Even with umbrellas, the three of them are drenched by the time they walk into the lobby.

"I'm glad we don't have the Spirits Tour tonight!" Sandy says.

"Yeah, good thing the séance is inside," Diane agrees.

Not surprisingly, the restaurant is mostly empty on this wet evening. They get seated at a table near the bar and peruse their menus. Their server brings some hand towels and a pot of hot coffee and some mugs so they can dry off and warm up a bit.

"That's better!" Ann says as she takes a sip of the fragrant, steaming coffee.

They start with the zucchini fritte, which is julienne style squash fried with a light breading, with marinara sauce for dipping. "These are delicious!" Diane says, as Sandy and Ann, mouths full of fritte, nod in agreement.

For the main course, they decide to go family style and order three different entrees and a bottle of red wine to pass around the table. Their choices are baked penne, chicken cacciatore, and lobster and shrimp fettucine. "This is fantastic!" Sandy raves. "Good choices, ladies."

"I love being able to sample everything!" Diane agrees.

There is a flash of lightning, followed by a loud crash of thunder, then the lights blink and go out. Several people gasp around the restaurant. Fortunately, there are enough lit candles on the tables that it's not completely black.

"OK, this is very creepy!" Ann says. The lights blink back on ten seconds later. "That's better!"

When their server comes back and asks them if they want dessert, all three of them groan and hold their tummies. "I'll take that as a no," he says and laughs. "Can I get you anything else?"

"No, just the check. Can you split it three ways?" Ann asks.

"Of course, Bella!" he replies.

The Colby Memorial Temple is only two blocks from the hotel, but it's still pouring out and lightning continues to crackle across the sky, so they drive to the temple. Even so, they are soaked once again by the time they get inside, and this time there are no towels or coffee. They are led back to the séance room by their host and find their seats at the table. Five other people are already seated. The room is quite cold, and several people are shivering.

"I'm going to turn the thermostat up so it's more comfortable in here," the host promises.

Sandy already feels bombarded by spirits trying to come through with messages. She feels them bouncing around in her brain and there are so many voices that she can't separate them to understand what they are saying. Over the years, she has discovered that she can shut them out to some degree through meditation. She visualizes a corner in her mind with a soft purple light surrounding it. When she crosses into the light, the spirits are unable to follow her there. Fortunately, the technique seems to be working for her as she practices it in this space.

Candles are lit around the room, and the Medium, Robyn, enters. She is dressed in a flowing black dress and has a colorful shawl, in shades of green, blue, and purple, wrapped around her shoulders. The electric lights are turned off, so the room is dimly lit by candlelight now. The participants are told that no photography or videotaping is permitted, but that the entire session will be recorded, and the audio file will be posted to a website that they will have access to in a few days.

The medium explains the tools they have around

the room and on the table to help them communicate with those who have crossed over. There are cat balls that light up and flashlights that can be turned on and off by those who have crossed over. There is an EVP, Electronic Voice Phenomenon, translator in the room that picks up electromagnetic communications from the spirits that are present. Robyn has placed tablets and pens at each table position and told the participants that they can take notes throughout the séance when they hear or learn anything that is interesting or relevant to them.

Another tool on the table are three pairs of metal rods that are bent at a ninety-degree angle. Robyn explains that they should be held parallel to each other, and when questions are asked of the spirits, they will move. If the rods remain parallel, the answer to the question is no. If the rods cross each other, that means yes. She asks two of the participants to pick them up and hold them parallel to each other, then try to make them move so they cross each other. It is impossible for them to control the movement using their hands. Robyn explains that the electromagnetic energy emitted by the spirits can easily move them, but a human cannot.

Each participant around the table introduces themselves, then Robyn asks them to join hands – right palm down, left palm up, and repeat several incantations after her.

"We surround ourselves with white light for our safety and protection." Those around the table repeat this statement. Robyn makes her way through the following statements as the participants repeat after her.

"No negative energy is welcome here."

"We come here with the utmost respect for the spirits of love and light."

"Please come forward and show yourselves now."

The room is no longer cold – it's a bit warm now with thirteen people crowded around the table in the small room. Robyn asks for silence and closes her eyes to allow herself to enter a meditative trance. The room suddenly becomes much colder.

"There are many spirits trying to come through. They have messages for you. I am going to take them one at a time. Please let me know if you have someone who has crossed over with the name or description as I call them out," Robyn tells them.

"I have a man named Frank who is insisting on being heard first. Who does this spirit belong to?" the Medium asks.

A woman at the table named Jenna gasps and puts her hand to her mouth. "I just lost my father two months ago," Jenna says. "I was in California on a work trip when it happened, and I couldn't make it back to the east coast to see him before he passed away. I feel so guilty that I didn't get to say goodbye."

A man's voice clearly comes across on the EVP translator, "Don't worry. I'm okay."

"Daddy?" Jenna asks.

"It's me," the voice replies. Jenna is laughing and crying at the same time.

"He doesn't want you to feel guilty, Jenna," Robyn tells her. "He knows that you love him and he's very proud of you. He wants you to be happy and know that you will see each other again in the spiritual plane." Jenna nods. "He also says you should get that puppy you've been admiring at the Pet Adoption Center and name it after him." Now Jenna is laughing even harder.

"I stopped there to look at that puppy every day this week," Jenna admits. "He's ornery just like my dad was. Guess I better adopt little Frank this week before someone else does!"

"Another spirit is here now. Jack. He's also somebody's dad. Who does he belong to?" Robyn asks.

"That's my dad!" Diane says.

"You two were very close – he says you were best friends after your mother died."

"Yes, we were," Diane admits.

"Jack wants you to know that all the love you have in this life continues with you into the next, and all the discontent and bad feelings evaporate."

Diane nods and says, "I really hope that is true!"

"He has a warning for you, though. This is extremely important and the reason he is here tonight."

Diane looks terrified. "What is it?"

"He says that it is good that you are helping your friend Ann, but the two of you will be in danger. Be very careful. He will be there with you, but you must always be cautious," Robyn tells them. Ann, Diane, and Sandy all look at each other in surprise. They were hoping for information about Andrew but weren't expecting to get a warning this evening.

"Is there anything else? What can we do to be safe?" Ann asks.

"He's gone," Robyn tells her.

A few more messages come in for other participants in the séance, including one from a pet for a man whose dog passed away unexpectedly. Nothing more comes through from Jack, and no messages are received from Ann's mother, Joan. Robyn turns the lights back on, and the girls are visibly disappointed that they didn't get something more concrete about Andrew.

"What's that?" Ann asks, pointing at the tablet in front of Sandy. Sandy looks down at the table and sees that she is holding a pen in her hand, and that she has written a street address on her tablet.

"I don't remember picking up the pen or writing anything!" Sandy gasps in surprise. "But that is my handwriting."

"Camelia Way," Ann reads from the tablet. "Do you think that is a street in Howey-in-the-Hills?"

Sandy picks up her phone to do a search on Google Maps but finds that her phone battery is completely drained. "That happens a lot in this room," Robyn remarks. "The spirits tend to take energy from anything electronic in the room, including batteries."

"I still have enough charge on mine," Diane says as she types in the address. "Yes, it's in Howey-in-the-Hills! We must have missed that area when we drove around there the other day."

"Can we go there now?" Ann asks.

"It's 49 miles from here – says it will take 57 minutes to get there. It's after 9 PM already...I don't think I have the energy for that tonight," Diane tells her.

"I'm exhausted – I'm with Diane," Sandy agrees.

"And your father warned us to be careful," Diane adds. "Going there in the middle of the night isn't my idea of being cautious!"

"You're right. But can we at least go first thing tomorrow morning?" Ann asks. "I really want to find Andrew, and we're so close now!"

Sandy and Diane agree to the plan, and they all return to Sandy's house to get a good night's rest.

Chapter 21

Despite feeling totally drained and exhausted, Sandy tosses and turns in her bed. The cats can sense her anxiety and are up on the bed with her. Timmy is lying on her chest, which he often does when she is anxious. The weight and warmth of him help to calm her down. Little Maceo is curled up by her head and licking her cheek. She's not sure if being overtired is the reason for her apprehensiveness, or if she is sensing impending trouble. Sandy carefully grabs her Kindle off the nightstand to avoid jostling the kitties and opens a nonfiction book on quantum physics. After a few minutes, she can barely keep her eyes open and nods off.

Sandy is outside of the Mediterranean Revival Style mansion that was in the picture that Ann's mother left at the wax museum. She's looking through the windows that are on the patio behind the house, trying to spot Andrew. Ann is right beside her peering through the same window. They are looking into a large dining room, and no one is in there. They hurry past a pair of glass doors to the next window. The window looks in on a family room with a huge gray wraparound sofa. A teenage boy is sitting on the sofa, and a furry orange tabby is sleeping on the cushion beside him.

"That's Andrew!" Ann says, a little too loudly. Both the boy and the cat startle and look toward the window. Sandy notices that the window is up, and that Andrew can hear them clearly through the screen.

Andrew stands up and shouts, "Nana! Someone is outside spying on us!"

Ann says, "Andrew, wait! I'm Ann...your sister!"

"I'm not Andrew. I don't have a sister. Get off our property!"

Nana enters the room and spots them through the window. Ann and Sandy take off running across the yard back to their car, which is parked on the side street. Uncle Ernie runs out the front door with a rifle in his hand. Diane, who was waiting for them in the car, stomps on the gas and squeals out into the street.

Sandy's heart is racing when she wakes up. She must have been thrashing around in the bed, because Mr. Tim is staring at her as if she's lost her mind, and Maceo is nowhere to be seen. She's still breathing heavy as the adrenaline courses through her bloodstream.

"I guess we need to come up with a better plan than sneaking around the house and peeping into the windows," Sandy tells Timmy.

"Prrrrrrrrt!" the cat chortles back at her.

"I know, you'd be out of luck if no one was here to feed you, you fat kitty." He looks away from her disdainfully as if he is offended by her fat-shaming of him. "I'm just teasing...you know I love a chubby kitty."

Sandy looks at the clock and sees that it's 2 AM. She's worried that she is too keyed up to get back to sleep, but when she closes her eyes and breathes deeply for a few breaths, she falls asleep again in no time.

***

Sandy wakes up with a start when she smells coffee brewing in the kitchen. She looks at the clock and is shocked to see that it's 9 AM! She never sleeps this late. She walks out to the kitchen, where Diane and Ann are dressed and drinking their coffee.

"Sorry, did we wake you?" Diane asks.

"No, but you should have! I never sleep this late!"

"You must have needed it," Ann tells her. "Rest when your body tells you to! By the way, I fed the kitties. Hope that's OK!"

"Yes, thanks for feeding them. They were probably starving since I am usually up no later than 7, and even earlier on workdays."

"Are we still going to Howey-in-the-Hills this morning?" Ann asks.

"Yes, just let me grab a quick shower and a bite

to eat, and I'll be ready. Give me fifteen minutes," Sandy says. "I think I had a dream about that house last night, but I can't remember it at all now."

About an hour later, Diane parks her car along the curb on the street near the house on Camelia Way. "What do we do now?"

"I want to go around the back and look in the windows," Ann says.

"I'll go with you," Sandy tells her.

"I'll wait in the car just in case we need to make a quick getaway," Diane teases.

Ann and Sandy scurry through the lawn, which is beautifully landscaped, with a lush green lawn, large mossy oak trees, and several varieties of palm trees. Around the back, there is a large patio with big arched windows. The first set of windows look in on a large dining room, but no one is in there. They move on to the next set of windows, which is the family room. Sandy sees Andrew, and her dream comes flooding back to her. Ann is opening her mouth to call out to her brother, and Sandy slaps her hand across her mouth and whispers to her, "Be quiet! We have to get out of here...I'll explain later."

Sandy drags Ann by the arm across the lawn and when they climb into the car, she says, "Diane, we need to get away from here quickly." Once they are safely on the road, Sandy explains her dream, and that she didn't remember any of it until it started happening exactly as she dreamt it.

"That was definitely Andrew," Ann says. "He's a lot bigger now, but it was him."

"Thank goodness you stopped her before she yelled for him!" Diane replies. "I would not be happy having to rush two bleeding friends to the hospital."

"Do you really think Uncle Ernie would have shot us?" Ann asks.

"I didn't want to stay to find out," Sandy says.

"What do we do now? I need to get in touch with my brother somehow."

"In my dream, he said his name isn't Andrew. I'm wondering if he's forgotten his past life with you?" Sandy explains. "In the first dream I had, the old woman, Nana, was trying to convince him that his name is Johnny. Maybe he only goes by that now."

"If Nana and Uncle Ernie kidnapped him, then they have a lot to lose if anyone finds out about it. We need to keep it to ourselves that we know who Andrew is until we have a chance to get him alone. And even then, we must be careful not to scare him off," Diane advises.

"I'm starving. Let's regroup at that cute German bakery we passed on the way here. Yalaha, I think it was called," Ann suggests.

"I'm hungry, too!" Sandy agrees. "That sounds great."

Chapter 22

"This place is adorable!" Diane says as they walk up to the tan, two-story structure with a red-tiled roof. "I didn't even notice it when we drove by earlier." The outside walls of Yalaha Bakery are decorated with 'Luftlmalerei' murals, which literally translates from German to English as 'airy paintings.' The arch above the double wooden door entryway has a painting in the style of a Bavarian coat-of-arms, with two standing lions holding a golden pretzel between them. Fruits, flowers, and grains decorate the murals on either side of the door.

"Look at these beautiful paintings," Sandy says, pointing to the murals across an archway to the left of the doors that leads into a courtyard. The archway is painted with a welcome sign surrounded by flowers and vines. In the courtyard there are iron bistro tables and chairs with white umbrellas for shade. "Let's get our food and bring it out here to eat."

There is a long line when they walk up to the bakery counter, and when they see the beautiful selection of baked goods behind the large glass display case, it's easy to see why. "Look at all this stuff!" Ann gushes. "How am I going to decide what to get? It all looks fantastic!"

"Get something for now, and take some home for later," Diane tells her. "That's what I'm going to do!"

The selection is truly amazing, with several varieties of fresh baked loaves of bread, soft pretzels called 'brezels', cakes, pies, streusels, cannoli, cream puffs, strudels, and eclairs. They choose their goodies and beverages, then make their way outside to the patio. The three of them picked something different to eat there so they can share and have a variety to sample right now. Ann chose the apple strudel, Sandy opted for a cream puff, and Diane chose a peach streusel.

"Oh, my goodness! Everything is delicious," Diane says. "Good thing I don't live near here. I'd be eating this every day." Ann and Sandy agree as they enjoy the tasty treats in the pleasantly shaded courtyard.

"I need to go to the bathroom before we drive back," Ann says.

"Me too," Sandy agrees, "And I want to get a couple things to take home with me for later." Ann and Diane nod vigorously.

The line isn't backed up now, so they have time to chat with the woman behind the counter. Sandy asks what the coat of arms with the lions holding the pretzel means. She tells them that the coat of arms is used widely across Europe to represent the pride and honor they have in their craft.

Ann asks, "What's the significance of the lions?"

"The story goes all the way back to 1510 AD, when the Ottoman Turks were attempting to take over Austria's capital, Vienna, by digging tunnels under the city walls. Monks, who were baking pretzels in the basement of their monastery late at night, heard them and stopped the attack. Because of their bravery, the Austrian emperor awarded them the coat of arms that you see outside our building."

"That's interesting! Thank you for sharing the history with us," Sandy tells the clerk. As they are waiting for their take-out items to be bagged up, a blond-haired boy walks into the bakery. "Ann, I think that's Andrew," Sandy whispers.

Ann turns to look at him. "That's definitely him! I need to talk to him."

"Wait! Make sure that Nana and Uncle Ernie aren't with him," Sandy warns her. They grab their goody bags and make their way to a table to sit down and surreptitiously watch Andrew. No one appears to be with him, and when he pulls a Yalaha apron out of his backpack and puts it on, they realize that he works here.

"He's here for his work shift," Ann says. "I'm going to go talk to him before he starts."

"OK, but remember, he doesn't go by Andrew

anymore! And he might not remember you, so don't scare him into thinking you are a crazy woman," Sandy cautions her.

Ann walks over to Andrew while Diane and Sandy wait at the table so as not to overwhelm him. "Hi, do you have a minute to talk to me?" Ann asks him.

"My shift doesn't start for 15 minutes, but I can answer any questions you have about the food and baked goods we sell here," Andrew, whose name tag says John, tells her.

"I know this is going to sound crazy, but I'm pretty sure I'm your older sister. My name is Ann." A flicker of recognition crosses Andrew's face, but he glances worriedly around to make sure that no one is listening. "When we lived together, we had an orange tabby cat named Freddie," Ann continues.

Andrew nods. "I have another cat named Freddie now, after the first cat. But I can't talk to you here. I will get in a lot of trouble if my Nana finds out." Andrew scribbles a phone number on a napkin. "This is my cell phone number. Call me at seven o'clock tomorrow night. Nana plays cards with her friends every Monday night." Ann nods, takes the napkin, and walks back to the table.

"What happened?" Diane whispers.

"He believes me, that I'm his sister, but he's worried about getting caught. He gave me his cell phone number and wants me to call him tomorrow night when his Nana will be out of the house."

"Wow, what a coincidence that we came here for some food!" Diane says.

"I don't believe in coincidences anymore. I think Ann and I noticed this place because someone out there is looking out for us – probably Joan or Jack." Ann nods her head and smiles.

"Aw, that would be just like my dad to help out," Diane agrees.

Chapter 23

There are no onsite meetings today for Project Dragonfly, so Ann and Diane went back to Cocoa Beach, and Sandy is working remotely from the townhouse in Orlando. She misses having their company and is thankful that at least the cats are with her. Dominic called her last night and is anxious for her and the cats to return home in a week and a half. Fortunately, the project is on schedule, so she doesn't expect her stay in Florida to be extended. Sandy is ready to go home but is hoping that she can help Ann resolve things with her brother before she heads back to Maryland.

Ann promised to update her and Diane after she talks to Andrew this evening. Sandy tries to focus on work and put it out of her mind for now. She gets so engrossed in her work that it's 2 PM before she realizes that she hasn't eaten anything yet today. Since she was busy all weekend, she never made it to the grocery store, so there's nothing left in the refrigerator except for two eggs. While she's boiling the eggs to make egg salad, she goes out to sit on the lanai by the pool and enjoy a bit of sunshine. Mr. Tim and Maceo quickly join her outside.

When the eggs are finished cooking, she toasts a couple slices of wheat bread, mixes the eggs with mayonnaise, and spreads it on the bread. She carries her plate outside. "Not a fancy meal, but tastes good," she tells the cats. They relax by the pool until 3 PM, then Sandy chases the cats inside so she can call in to her next meeting.

***

Sandy's phone rings that evening, and she answers immediately when she sees that it's Ann calling. "Hey, Ann. What's up?"

"I talked to Andrew. He remembers being kidnapped, and being locked in the attic when he was five years old. He's been too terrified to do anything about it – he had no way of finding us and nowhere to go."

"That's awful!' Sandy says.

"He's being abused by Nana and Uncle Ernie. They force him to work on Ernie's fishing boat or in the bakery when he's not in school. He must hand over any money that he makes to Nana. His grades are poor because he doesn't have time to do his homework, and he's not allowed to spend time with any of his school friends or do extracurricular activities," Ann explains. "They treat him like a servant, not a son."

"What are you going to do?"

"He has to come live with me," Ann says.

"Are you sure you are ready to take care of a teenager?" Sandy asks her.

"He's my brother! I have to take care of him," Ann says. "I *want* to take care of him."

"Yes, you're right. I'd feel the same way. But won't they report it as a kidnapping?"

"Andrew is willing to tell the police everything, but he has to feel safe before he can do that. And a DNA test will quickly prove that we are siblings."

"So, what's the plan?" Sandy asks.

"Andrew is working at the bakery tomorrow night. He's going to shove as much of his clothes and belongings into his backpack that will fit and take it to Yalaha. He'll leave all his schoolbooks and notebooks in his locker at school, and we'll decide what to do with them later. His shift is from four to nine o'clock tomorrow evening, but he's going to say he's sick and leave at seven. I'll be waiting in the parking lot for him."

"Do you want me to come along?" Sandy asks.

"No, I can handle it. I'll be careful," Ann says.

"OK. Please call me if you change your mind, or need help with anything," Sandy tells her.

"Will do."

Chapter 24

Ann took a half day off work so she can get the apartment ready for Andrew, and make sure she is at Yalaha by 6:30 PM. The bakery is a 95-minute drive from Cocoa Beach with no traffic, so she needs to allow two hours for the drive at rush hour. Her guest bedroom is currently acting as a storage room, so she moves out the boxes, and picks up the clothes that are piled up on the bed and throws them into a big garbage bag to be sorted out later to keep, donate, or toss away. She moves the clothes out of the closet and moves them into her bedroom closet for sorting as time permits.

The sheets have been on the full-size bed for over a year, when her college roommate visited from Virginia. She strips them off and throws them into the washing machine. It will be an adjustment having another person in her small apartment, but they will figure it out.

Ann arrives at Yalaha Bakery at 6:25 PM. She waits in the car, fiddling with her phone, then trying to read a book, until 7:00. She looks expectantly at the door. Andrew should be coming out any minute. Five minutes go by, then ten, then fifteen –

still no sign of Andrew. Where is he?

After twenty minutes pass, Ann walks into the bakery to look for him. She goes up to the counter, and a young girl greets her and asks how she can help her.

"I'm here to pick up John. Do you know where he is?" Ann asks her.

"He didn't come in tonight," she tells Ann.

"Did he call in sick?"

"No, nobody heard from him. He just didn't show up. We tried to call him at home, but nobody picked up the phone."

Now Ann is worried. Did Nana discover their plan? Ann calls his cell phone, hoping there has been some mix-up.

"Who is this?" a gruff male voice growls into the phone. It's not Andrew's voice. Ann quickly hangs up. She immediately calls Sandy.

"Hi, Ann. Is everything OK?" Sandy asks.

"No! Andrew didn't show up for work. I am so worried. Someone else answered his cell phone when I tried to call him. I think it was Uncle Ernie. I'm afraid he and Nana know what we are trying to do," Ann confesses. "I'm going over to their house to try to find him."

"No, don't do that, Ann. It's not safe! Wait until he reaches out to you again. He has your number. He will find a way."

"I guess you're right. I'm so worried about him though."

"I know, sweetie, but we know they are not nice people. You can't help Andrew if something happens to you. Promise me you will wait until you hear from him."

"OK," Ann says reluctantly. "I'll keep you posted when I hear something."

"Thank you! Try to get some rest tonight," Sandy tells her.

"I will," Ann says, knowing full well that she is not going to sleep a wink until she rescues Andrew, and she's going to go there tonight to do it.

***

Ann drives to the house where Andrew lives and parks on the street several houses away. She is thankful that it's a dark night, with no moon, and that there aren't many streetlights along the way. She creeps as stealthily as possible to the back of the house and looks in the family room window. It's dark – no sign of Andrew. Ann jumps when she hears a twig snap behind her, and before she can turn around to look, there is a hand over her mouth, and she is being dragged roughly across the yard. She throws her weight backward on the man who has hold of her and knocks him off balance enough that she is able to escape his grip and start running. The man catches her, tackles her to the ground, then hits her on the head with something heavy. Everything goes black.

Andrew, watching from the attic window, sees what's happening. Uncle Ernie drags Ann by her arms across the lawn to his car in the driveway, opens the trunk, and tosses her in. "Poor Ann!" Andrew thinks to himself. "She was only trying to help me, and now my uncle is hurting her. He may have already killed her." Tears stream down his face. He has been in the attic since Nana found the messages and calls between him and Ann on his phone early this morning. She took his phone away, so there was no way he could warn Ann that they were onto the plan. Nana locked him in the room where he was kept after he was kidnapped, and he hasn't had anything to eat or drink since last night. He should have known better than to try to escape. Now they're going to kill Ann and probably him, too.

Andrew hears a faint meowing from the back corner of the room. "Freddie? Is that you?" The meowing gets louder. He walks over and finds a large crack between the floorboards. It's very dark, so he can't see much through the crack, but Freddie is sticking his nose through it. When Andrew puts his fingers through the crack, Freddie promptly licks them with his rough kitty tongue.

***

When Ann wakes up, her head is pounding and her whole body aches. When she tries to roll over, she realizes that her arms are tied behind her at the wrists, and her legs are tied at the ankles. Then she remembers being hit on the head while looking for Andrew. It's very dark in here, but she can feel a rocking motion, so she believes that she is on a boat – probably Uncle Ernie's boat. She smells the fishy aroma of the sea.

Ann pulls her knees into her chest, then uses her tied arms to lever herself into a sitting position. She looks around to check if she can see anything. There appears to be a high window about ten feet away with a bit of light coming through. Ann rocks forward and back on her butt until she gets enough momentum to stand on her feet. She loses her balance the first time, since standing on tied feet is difficult, but the second time she does it, she is able to stand. Thank goodness for the yogalates classes she has been taking for the last few months. It's really improved her core strength! She's able to shuffle from side to side to move herself forward slowly toward the window. When she is almost there, her legs bump against something. She turns to the side so she can feel it and finds a mattress. The window must be right above the bed. She carefully sits down on it and maneuvers herself as close to the window as she can. The window is fixed in place and isn't designed to open. When she looks out, she sees that the boat is docked, and there aren't any other boats nearby. So much for trying to pound the window and scream for help.

Her head is throbbing like crazy, so she lies down on the bed to rest, and is out again in a matter of seconds.

Chapter 25

Diane is sleeping in her apartment in Cocoa Beach when she is startled awake by the sound of the television. She knows she didn't leave the TV on when she went to bed – how did it get turned on? She grabs the remote control off her nightstand, points it at the TV and turns it off. Just as she is dozing off again, the TV comes back on. Now she is scared. Who is in her room?

"Who's there?" she yells. "Don't come near me, I have a gun!" Diane doesn't have a gun. She's never even held a gun, but she's scared and grasping at straws. Although why would someone who wants to murder her turn the TV on first? She squints at the television, and sees the face of Jack, her father, there.

"Hi sweetheart, it's me. Don't be afraid. The only way I can talk to you is by manipulating electromagnetic energy using the television as a receiver," her dad tells her.

"Daddy, what are you doing here?" Diane asks him. "Wait, is that Joan beside you?" The face of Joan, Ann's mom, has materialized on the TV beside Jack's face.

"Yes, it's me, honey. Ann is in trouble. Uncle Ernie caught her trying to rescue Andrew and has her tied up in the hull of his fishing boat. If you look at your phone, you'll see that I sent the location to your GPS."

"Don't go alone, though," Jack warns. "Take someone with you and be careful." The television turns itself off.

"WTF!" Diane shouts at the blank TV. "Who am I going to call and ask to help me with something two dead people told me to do?" Then she realizes that Sandy is the only one she can call, since she knows the whole story.

Sandy picks up on the first ring. "That was quick! Why are you up so late?" Diane asks her. It's nearly midnight.

"I was feeling very anxious - I have a bad feeling about Ann. She was supposed to pick up Andrew at Yalaha tonight, and he didn't show up."

"That's exactly why I'm calling. She's in trouble!" Diane says.

"How do you know?"

"My dad and Joan showed up on my TV and told me!" Diane replies. "I know that sounds crazy, but they showed me exactly where she is. Uncle Ernie has her."

"No, it doesn't sound crazy at all. Give me the address, and I'll meet you there."

***

"How did you get up here, Freddie?" Andrew asks the cat, as he pets him through the crack in the floor. If he made it up here, there must be a way down. Andrew searches around the room for anything he can use to pry up the floorboard. He remembers that the cot he is sleeping on has metal slats underneath. He pulls the mattress off the metal frame and is happy to find that the metal slats slide into the frame and are not welded in place. He can work one of them out to use as a lever.

"Get back, Freddie. I don't want to poke you in the eye," Andrew tells the kitty. The cat understands 'get back' and moves away from the hole. It takes several attempts, since the metal slat is not quite stiff enough, but he finally works the board loose and is able to lift it out. Freddie promptly jumps through the hole and into the attic, as Andrew looks down onto a set of narrow stairs. "I never knew there was a second staircase in this house! Good kitty, Freddie," Andrew says and scratches Freddie under the chin. He works quickly to remove two more boards from the opening, which should be enough for him to squeeze through.

Andrew lowers himself, feet first, through the hole, scratching his bare legs on the splintered boards, until he is sitting on a step below. He scoots his butt down a few more steps until he can stand up, then follows the stairs to the second floor.

He opens a small door on the landing and enters a section of the house he has never seen before. There are two small bedrooms, one with a crib and another with a small bed like the one he was sleeping on in the attic. He knew he wasn't crazy! There *were* other children crying here. Freddie follows him and sniffs the bed clothes and the stuffed animals that are strewn about the room.

Andrew hears footsteps, and quickly goes back to the stairs and descends to the first floor. The small door opens into a very small, dark room. It takes him a moment to figure out that he is inside the kitchen pantry. He's lived here for nine years and never realized that this staircase or the secret bedrooms were here. He listens for a few minutes to determine if Nana is in the kitchen. When he doesn't hear anything, he pushes open the pantry door, creeps over to the back door in the kitchen, and takes off running across the lawn.

Chapter 26

Forty-five minutes later, both Diane and Sandy are at the dock. "Joan said that Ann is in the hull of Ernie's boat. There's only one boat here. That must be it," Diane whispers to Sandy. Diane starts to move toward the boat, but Sandy grabs her arm to stop her.

"Let's make sure Ernie isn't watching. It won't do Ann any good if he shoots us on the way to rescuing her." They watch from the edge of the water, where they are in the shadows. There is a light on the dock illuminating the walkway, but no lights are on in the boat, and they don't hear any sounds coming from the vessel. They wait quietly for about ten minutes, then decide to stealthily approach the boat.

Fortunately, the water is calm, so the boat isn't rocking too much. Sandy gives Diane her hand for balance as she steps on deck, then Diane helps pull Sandy onto the boat. "Here's the hatch that goes below," Diane whispers. She gives it a tug, and they can see the steps leading down to the hull.

Ann hears the movement on the stairs, and shouts, "Who's there?"

"Shhh! It's me and Sandy. Is Ernie here?" Diane says.

"Oh! I have never been happier to see you two! I don't think he's here. I've been down in this hole by myself for hours," Ann tells them. "How on earth did you find me?"

"Jack and Joan told me where you are! Through my TV."

"Huh?"

"We'll explain later, but right now, we have to get you out of here," Sandy says, as she finds the light switch and the cabin illuminates. She tries to undo the ropes that are binding Ann's arms and legs, but the knots are too tight. Diane sees a small kitchen toward the front of the hull and checks the drawers for something sharp.

"I found a steak knife!" she says as she carries it over and hands it to Sandy. Sandy carefully slides it under the rope, being careful not to cut Ann, and starts sawing back and forth. It's a heavy-duty rope, so it takes a couple minutes to completely cut through it.

"That feels so good!" Ann says as she rubs her wrists and stretches out her hands. Sandy is now feverishly sawing at the rope around her ankles.

There is loud stomping on the deck above. "Shit, Ernie is back!" Ann whispers. Unfortunately, the rope around her legs is still not cut loose as he stomps down the steps. Sandy sticks the knife in the back of her shorts to hide it from Ernie.

"What the hell is going on here?" he shouts, pulling out his gun and pointing it at the three of them.

***

Andrew overheard Nana telling Uncle Ernie to take his sister to the boat, kill her, and throw her into the deepest part of the lake. It's about five miles to where his uncle docks his boat, so he grabs his bike and pedals as fast as he can to the lake. He knows that Ann's life is at stake if he doesn't make it in time.

The lights are on in the hull, and he hears shouting coming from the boat. Andrew has no idea what he's going to do now. He was in such a rush to get here that he didn't think about bringing a weapon with him. He looks around the dock to see if there is anything he can use to fight his uncle. There is a small rowboat tied on the other side of the dock. He creeps over to it, and searches for anything he can use to defend himself. There is a small steel anchor on the floor of the boat – he can easily lift it, but it is heavy enough that he could knock Uncle Ernie out if he hit him on the head.

Andrew makes his way over to Ernie's boat, carrying the anchor, and tiptoes across the deck and down the stairs as quietly as possible. His uncle has a gun pointed at his sister and two other women that he recognizes from the bakery. Ann's eyes widen as she sees Andrew at the top of the steps. Trying to create a distraction so that Ernie doesn't hear her brother, Ann falls backward and lands on the floor with a thud.

"Get up, bitch!" Ernie screams at her. This gives Andrew just enough time to swing the anchor and club Ernie across the back of the head. Ernie immediately crumples to the floor. He's out cold.

Andrew runs over to Ann and she pulls him into a hug. "Are you OK?" he asks her.

"Yes, I'm fine. Are you OK? How on earth did you find us?" she asks her brother.

"I'm OK. I heard Nana telling Uncle Ernie to bring you here. He was going to kill you!"

"Yeah, I figured that was his plan," Ann replies.

"Let's finish untying your legs," Sandy says, as she pulls the knife out from her shorts. The rope falls away and Ann stands up again.

"Ouch, I think I cracked my tailbone when I did my stunt fall," Ann says.

"That was a really good distraction, though!" Diane tells her.

"Can you walk?" Sandy asks her.

"Yeah, walking is fine. Sitting might be a problem."

Ernie hasn't moved at all since Andrew clobbered him with the anchor. "Do you think I killed him?"

he asks. "Am I going to go to jail?"

"No, that was definitely self-defense!" Ann tells him.

Sandy walks over and checks Ernie for breathing and a pulse. "He's not dead. I'll call 9-1-1 to get some help, and we can report Andrew's kidnapping, and what he did to Ann." She pulls out her cell phone. "Crap, I don't have a signal. Diane, is your phone working?"

"No signal here, either," she tells them.

"Ernie took my phone," Ann says.

"I don't have mine either," Andrew says. "Nana took it away from me and locked me in the attic when she saw our texts. Sometimes the signal is better up on deck."

They climb up out of the hull, and Sandy checks her phone again. "You're right. I have a decent signal now. Just as she starts to dial 9-1-1, a figure steps out of the shadows.

"Drop your phone, or I'll shoot." Nana is five feet away and has her gun pointed straight at them.

Ann makes a lunge for Nana, thinking that this old woman can be easily overtaken by the four of them. Nana promptly shoots Ann in the foot.

"Mother Fucker!" Ann shouts. She falls back on her butt and hits her tailbone. "Fuck!"

"I'm not kidding. Get back now or I'll shoot every

one of you. You are trespassing on my property. It's my legal right to shoot you. Put your hands in the air."

They all put their hands up. Sandy wishes that she had put the steak knife back in her pants, but she left it lying on the floor under the deck. The temperature suddenly drops 20 degrees and Sandy sees that Joan and Jack are here, floating behind Nana. She glances over at Diane, and she can see that Diane sees them, too. Ann is moaning in pain beside her, so she whispers to Ann that her mom is with them, and they'll get some help for her soon.

"Get away from her – stop whispering or you're the next to get it!" Nana screams. Joan flies in front of Nana, creating a huge gust of wind that knocks her off balance. Her gun falls to the deck, and before she can grab it, Jack swoops in from the other side and Nana is pushed over the edge of the boat and lands with a splash in the water.

Sandy grabs the gun. "Andrew, go look for a belt or something we can use as a tourniquet for Ann's leg to cut off the blood flow. Also, bring a towel." Andrew climbs down the steps to look for the items. "Diane, does your phone have a signal now? Can you call 9-1-1?"

"Yes, I have a signal. I'm on it," Dianereplies.

Andrew comes back with a towel and some of the rope that was used to tie Ann up. "I couldn't find a belt. Will this work?" he says as he holds up the rope.

"Yes, that will do. Put pressure on her foot where the bullet entered to stop the blood flow," Sandy directs him, as she ties the rope tightly around Ann's calf to stop the blood flow.

"Ouch, that's too tight!" Ann says.

"Good, that means it's tight enough to keep you from losing blood," Sandy tells her.

"The ambulance is on the way!" Diane reports. "They'll be here in five minutes. Hang on, Ann!"

Andrew looks up and sees Joan hovering above Ann. "Is that Mom?" he whispers.

Ann looks up and sees her too. "Yes! Mom – I miss you so much!" Joan materializes to the point where she is no longer transparent and puts her arms around her son and daughter. Jack fades away as Joan becomes more solid. Sandy guesses that he is transferring his energy to Joan so she can be more fully present with her children for a few fleeting moments.

Chapter 27

Ann is recovering from her foot surgery and has a donut pillow to allow her tailbone to heal. Fortunately, Andrew has now moved in with her, and helps her get around. She has approval from NASA to work from home until her foot is healed. Diane stops by several times a week to bring groceries or anything else they need until Ann gets back to driving again.

When the police arrested Nana, whose full name is Harriet Hornblatt, and her son, Ernie Hornblatt, Andrew and Ann explained that Andrew had been kidnapped nine years ago and kept locked in the attic. Andrew told them that over the years, he heard other children's voices from the attic and the other secret rooms that he found off the back staircase. The house was searched, and DNA was discovered from seven different children that had disappeared from the area over the past ten years. Harriet and Ernie are being held for charges of kidnapping and questioned about what happened to the children.

Freddie has happily adjusted to his new home in Ann's apartment. Just like Andrew, Ann loves him as much as she loved the first Freddie, too.

Sandy is back home in Ellicott City. Ann sees her on Zoom calls frequently and they also touch base often so Ann can fill her in on her recovery and on the status of the ongoing investigation of the kidnappings.

***

Timmy and Maceo are happy to be back in the big old house in Maryland. The townhouse in Orlando was fun, but they didn't have as much room to run around and chase each other. Dominic is ecstatic to have the three of them home. He expected to miss Sandy but didn't realize how much he would miss the furballs.

The four of them are enjoying the balmy day on the roof deck. "I can't believe how nice the weather is today!" Sandy gushes. Surprisingly mild for the beginning of April, the day is sunny and clear, with just wispy clouds in the sky. It's warm enough to be in shorts and t-shirts. "It would be really tough to come back from Florida and still have snow on the ground."

"We don't get snow in April too often in Maryland," Dom laughs.

"No, but I remember a blizzard or two that hit that late in the season."

The white and pink blossoms have already opened on the pear and cherry trees, and the tulips and daffodils are blooming. "I'm happy that I didn't have to be in Florida for work any longer than I did. I'd hate to miss spring!" Timmy and Maceo are batting dead leaves, the last signs of the passing winter, around the deck.

"Yeah, we have a beautiful spring season in Baltimore and D.C.," Dominic agrees. "So, you're not happy to be back because you missed me terribly?"

"Of course I am! And I did. Especially when I had to clean up the kitchen myself," she teases. Dom cleans up the kitchen every morning, usually before Sandy is even out of bed.

"Well, it's good to be missed for something," he says as he rolls his eyes.

"That's not the only thing I missed," Sandy says, as she slowly moves her hand down his chest, then his abdomen, and down to his crotch.

"Hey, not in front of the cats!" he says in mock horror.

Sandy wraps her arms around her husband and kisses him passionately. "I missed everything about you." She grabs his hand and leads him back into the house.

"C'mon, cats," Dom says, and they both come running in behind them. Sandy drags Dom into the bedroom and closes the door behind him before the cats can follow them in.

***

Ann walks into Andrew's bedroom and finds him sobbing on his bed. Freddie Krueger Fluffovich, II is curled up beside Andrew, licking his hand, as if he is trying to comfort the boy.

"What's wrong, honey?" Ann asks as she puts her arms around her brother.

"I did something really bad," he tells her.

"It can't be that bad. You can tell me anything," she reassures him.

"It's really bad...it's terrible. I'm afraid I'm going to be put in jail with Nana and Uncle Ernie."

"Andrew, what is it?"

"Those kids that went missing from our town? Nana paid me to bring kids home with me and play with them. She told me that she took them back to their homes afterward, but I know she didn't. I never saw any of them again after that. I know they were the ones that I heard crying from the attic and the other secret rooms."

"You were kidnapped, honey. They had control over you and threatened you. No one would hold you responsible for that," Ann tries to reassure him.

"They would lock me in the attic for days with no food when I didn't do what they wanted me to do. They told me to buddy up with kids on the playground who weren't being watched by their parents. I'd tell them I had candy and lots of toys at home. Some kids were smart enough not to come, but there were a lot of them who weren't."

"Do you remember their names? And what they looked like?" Ann asks him.

"Yeah, some of them."

"How many did you bring home?"

"Nine or ten," Andrew says, and starts sobbing again.

"I know you're upset and blaming yourself, but this isn't your fault. We really should report this to the police, honey. It could help them find where they are now and bring closure to their families."

Andrew nods and wipes away his tears. "I know. It's the right thing to do. I'm just really scared."

"You are a minor, and you were being threatened by adults. No one is going to blame you."

"What if they're dead? It's all my fault."

"No, it's Nana and Ernie's fault. This isn't on you, Andrew. But we need to do what we can to help now that you are safe." Andrew nods again. He knows his sister is right.

Chapter 28

With the additional information that Andrew provided, the search of the Hornblatt property turned up DNA from sixteen missing children from the area. Harriet and Ernie admitted to human trafficking, targeting children under twelve years old who are being sold for child sex and pornography. Andrew was able to provide descriptions for several of the victims. Unfortunately for the majority, the kidnapping occurred years ago, and the trail is cold. But there are two recent cases where investigators were able to follow the chain of sale and recover the children, who were returned to their parents. As expected, the detective recognized that Andrew was coerced into helping his kidnappers and no blame was placed upon him.

"I know it was awful for you to be kidnapped and held hostage for all these years," Ann tells Andrew. "But it really is a miracle that you weren't sold. We probably would have never found you!"

"Yes, I am lucky when I think about what happened to the other kids," Andrew says with tears in his eyes. "Nana often said that the only reason she kept me was because I had pretty blue eyes and blond hair that reminded her of her son, Johnny, who died in a car accident when he was only six years old. That's why she called me Johnny."

"I'm so happy that we are finally together as a family," Ann tells him as she wraps her arms around him and kisses his forehead. "It's too bad that it didn't happen before Mom died – she loved you so much." Andrew nods, and the tears are streaming down his cheeks now. "But she was with us at the boat, and she knows you are safe now."

"So that really happened? I thought maybe it was just a dream. I could really feel her hugging me."

"Yes, it was real. She materialized before us for just a few moments, then she disappeared. I know she was still on this earthly plane to help me find you."

"I hope she can find peace now," Andrew says.

"Me too," Ann agrees. "I read that if you ask a loved one for a sign, they can let you know they are OK. But you need to ask for something specific – something that you wouldn't see every day. Don't tell anyone what you wished for until after you receive it."

"OK. I am thinking of something specific. I'll let you know if she sends it to me."

The sign Andrew requested from his mother is a double rainbow. It holds significance for him because it takes him back to a special day that just he and his mother spent together. Joan let him take off school for the day – it was his birthday – and he was allowed to pick whatever he wanted to do for the day. They went to his favorite playground so he could play on the swings, slide, and jungle gym. He was sad because it started to rain, then pour, and they had to take refuge under the picnic pavilion. But the rain only lasted for fifteen minutes, then the sun came out, brightly shining through the remaining drops of rain. His mother pointed out the beautiful, double rainbow in the sky. She told him to remember when things look bad, that there is always a rainbow on the other side letting you know that everything will get better again.

***

Andrew is very nervous today. He must go to a new school in Cocoa Beach for the first time. He doesn't know anyone! But he is relieved that he doesn't have to face anyone at his old school in Howey-in-the-Hills. Everyone has heard about the kidnappings by now and that Nana and Ernie are in jail. Even though they weren't his blood relatives, he doesn't want to be associated with them in any way going forward.

He walks into the school, finds his way to his eighth-grade homeroom. The teacher welcomes him and tells him he can sit anywhere. He goes to the back of the room where he can be as inconspicuous as possible. The other kids file in and don't really notice him, which is what he was hoping for. A cute girl with short, curly black hair and bright blue eyes walks in just as the bell is ringing. She catches sight of him, gives him a big, bright smile, and takes the desk right beside his.

"Hi, I'm Jo – short for Joanna. Are you new here?" she says as she extends her hand to Andrew.

"Yes, I'm Andrew," he says as he takes her hand and shakes it. "This is my first day here. I just moved here from Orlando." No one knows Howey-in-the-Hills, so he just tells her the closest city that she's heard of.

"It's nice to meet you!" Jo puts her backpack down on her desk, and Andrew notices that it has a unicorn on it, and behind the unicorn is a double rainbow.

"Thanks, Mom!" he says silently to himself.

Chapter 29

Sandy is on a Zoom call with Diane and Ann to prep for the customer design review coming up next week. They are right on schedule and slightly under budget for the design of the spectrometer that will be used to measure the surface composition of Titan. They spend an hour nailing down status and remaining actions needed to be done prior to CDR. Once they finish their work discussion, they spend a few minutes chatting about what happened in Orlando and the status of the investigation into the kidnappings. Sandy is relieved to hear that the trafficking chain has been disrupted and the major players have been charged with felonies. Ann lets them know that her foot is healing well, and that Andrew is adjusting to his new school. Her brother is getting counseling for the trauma he experienced with Nana and Uncle Ernie. She tells them that he even has his first girlfriend, Jo.

When Sandy gets off the call, she rushes home to get ready for a night out with Dom, Rita, and Kevin. She hasn't seen Rita since she left for Florida and can't wait to catch up with her.

They meet for drinks and dinner at UMI Sushi on Main Street in old Ellicott City. Rita grabs Sandy and pulls her in for a big hug. "I missed you so much!"

"Me too!" Sandy agrees. "It's so wonderful to see you."

The mild weather has continued, so they get a table shaded by a pretty, red umbrella on the outside deck. Dom and Kevin get IPAs, and Rita gets the Tokyo Express, which has sake, plum wine, and peach Schnapps in it, and Sandy opts for the Kiss Dragon, with Tequila, Triple Sec, orange and pineapple juice. They start with shrimp dumplings and edamame appetizers.

"How's little Davey doing?" Sandy asks Rita. "Who's watching him tonight?"

"He's great!" Rita tells her. "Kevin's mom has him tonight."

"Davey's getting into everything these days," Kevin adds. "His favorite game is chasing Tutti around the house. She loves it, too, and it's great exercise for her."

"How's your new kitten doing?" Rita asks. "How did he do on the drive from Orlando?"

"He's really cute," Sandy replies. "Timmy and Maceo were both great on the drive home. I barely heard a squeak out of them! It's like they could sense that we were heading back to their big house in Maryland."

"Did you make good progress on Dragonfly while you were there?" Kevin asks Sandy.

"Yes, it was a productive trip, workwise. And of course, I got up to some ghost adventures as well." Sandy fills them in on everything that happened in Florida, most of which Dom had already heard about. "Enough about me. How is your triathlon training coming along, Kevin?"

"Dom has me on a tough schedule!" Kevin admits. "I was working out, either a swim, bike, or run, seven days a week. Now I'm up to two workouts on Wednesday, Saturday, and Sunday. Your husband is a tyrant!"

"He always has been very disciplined about his training," Sandy laughs. "I'm sure you two are going to do great in November."

"We'll see!" Kevin says.

"You have a huge wingspan, so you're going to kill it in the swim," Dom tells him.

"As long as I get used to swimming in the ocean and not letting the waves push me off course. I need to practice that more."

They're all hungry for sushi tonight, so they opt for a sushi boat they can share. The Tsunami Boat is the one they choose, and it comes out with an assortment of ten rolls.

"Yum! This is delicious," Rita says.

"Fabulous!" Sandy agrees.

"Oh, I talked to Jennifer a couple days ago," Rita tells Sandy. Jennifer is their friend from Georgia that they met in college.

"That's nice! I haven't talked to her in ages. How is she doing?"

"She's moving to Charleston!"

"What? Jennifer and Jason just fixed up that house in Savannah!" Sandy replies.

"Yeah, she got a promotion, but she had to move to Charleston. She's excited about it."

"What about Jason?" Jennifer hired Jason a year ago to oversee the renovations on the historic home she bought in Savannah a year ago. They hit it off and have been inseparable ever since.

"He moved to Charleston too! He can run his contracting business from anywhere. They just got engaged."

"Wow! All kinds of news from Jennifer."

"Oh, and guess what. This house is old and haunted, too," Rita tells Sandy. The two of them helped Jennifer figure out who was haunting her house in Savannah. "She wants us to come down and help with spirit wrangling…"

"Here we go again," Kevin says. Dominic just shakes his head.

Acknowledgement

Many thanks, as always, to my wonderful sister and editor, Lucy Sgrignoli. Her patience is endless, and I would not be a writer without her.

Thanks also to my husband, kids, and other traveling companions, who make visiting the places that I write about even more fun.

About The Author

Maria Difrancesco

Maria loves books, ghost stories, and cats. She studied engineering in college, much to the disappointment of her high school English teacher, who thought she should be a writer.  After spending many years working in engineering and management at large corporations, Maria decided to write her first novel, Ellicott City Ghost Story.

Maria has two grown children, and lives with her husband and two cats in Ellicott City, Maryland.

Books By This Author

Ellicott City Ghost Story

Cambridge Ghost Story

Catonsville Ghost Story

New Smyrna Beach Ghost Story

Maria And Sofia: A Ghost Story

Narragansett Ghost Story

Sarasota Ghost Story

Savannah Ghost Story

Made in the USA
Columbia, SC
28 July 2024

39517368R00098